FROM THE PAGES OF CANDIDE

In this best of all possible worlds the baron's castle was the most magnificent of all castles, and my lady the best of all possible baronesses.   (page 12)

Candide was struck with amazement and really could not conceive how he came to be a hero.   (page 15)

"If this is the best of all possible worlds, what are the others like?"
(page 29)

"A modest woman may be once violated, but her virtue is greatly strengthened as a result."   (page 33)

"In the different countries in which it has been my fate to wander, and the many inns where I have been a servant, I have observed a prodigious number of people who held their existence in abhorrence, and yet I never knew more than twelve who voluntarily put an end to their misery."   (page 50)

"Never while I live shall I lose the remembrance of that horrible day on which I saw my father and brother barbarously butchered before my eyes, and my sister ravished."   (page 59)

"In this country it is necessary, now and then, to put one admiral to death in order to inspire the others to fight."   (page 100)

"Our labour keeps us from three great evils—boredom, vice, and want."   (page 129)

"We must cultivate our garden."   (page 130)

DR. PANGLOSS SURVEYS THE WORLD.

CANDIDE,
OR OPTIMISM

Voltaire

With an Introduction and Notes by Gita May

Translated by Henry Morley
Translation revised by Lauren Walsh
Illustrated by Alan Odle

George Stade
Consulting Editorial Director

BARNES & NOBLE CLASSICS
NEW YORK

$\mathcal{JB}$

BARNES & NOBLE CLASSICS

NEW YORK

Published by Barnes & Noble Books
122 Fifth Avenue
New York, NY 10011

www.barnesandnoble.com/classics

Candide was first published in French in 1759.
Henry Morley's translation was first published in 1922.

Published in 2003 by Barnes & Noble Classics with new
Introduction, Notes, Biography, Chronology, Inspired By,
Comments & Questions, and For Further Reading.

Introduction, Notes, and For Further Reading
Copyright © 2003 by Gita May.

Note on Voltaire, The World of Voltaire and *Candide*,
Inspired by *Candide*, and Comments & Questions
Copyright © 2003 by Barnes & Noble, Inc.

Candide
ISBN-13: 978-1-59308-028-0
ISBN-10: 1-59308-028-X
LC Control Number 2003102532

Produced and published in conjunction with:
Fine Creative Media, Inc.
322 Eighth Avenue
New York, NY 10001

Michael J. Fine, President and Publisher

Printed in the United States of America
QM
30   29

VOLTAIRE

François-Marie Arouet (pen name "Voltaire") was born in Paris on November 21, 1694, into a middle-class family. His formal education took place at the Jesuit Collège Louis-le-Grand, where he studied Latin and Greek literature and drama. Despite his father's wish that he pursue a career in the law, he chose to devote himself to writing. After completing his education, François began moving in radical political circles and became infamous in Paris as a brilliant and sarcastic wit. For allegedly penning two libelous poems about the French regent, the duke of Orleans, he was imprisoned in the Bastille; during an eleven-month detention he completed his first dramatic tragedy, *Oedipe*, which was a critical success, and around this same time adopted the pen name "Voltaire."

When threatened with imprisonment for a second time, Voltaire instead chose exile to England, where he lived for two and a half years. He carefully studied English society and was particularly impressed by the constitutional monarchy and the religious freedom the English enjoyed, which he praised in *Letters Concerning the English Nation* (1733). When this work was published in French the following year as *Lettres philosophiques*, it was interpreted as critical of the French government and caused a great stir. Voltaire left Paris and spent the next fifteen years at the estate of his mistress, Madame du Châtelet. During this time, he published *Elements de la philosophie de Newton* (*Elements of Newton's Philosophy*; 1738), was appointed the royal historiographer of France, and was elected to the prestigious French Academy. During the early 1750s he was associated with the court of Frederick the Great in Prussia; while there he published the historical work *Le siècle de Louis XIV* (*The Age of Louis XIV*; 1751).

Two great events of the mid-1750s have a profound effect on Voltaire. Tens of thousands of people were killed in a great earthquake in Lisbon in 1755, and in 1756 the devastating Seven Years War began. Influenced in part by these events, Voltaire came to reject the philosophy of German philosopher Gottfried Wilhelm Leibniz, which was based on the concept of a rational and well-regulated universe. In 1759 Voltaire retreated to Ferney, an estate near the France-Switzerland border, where he wrote philosophical poems, letters, and narratives, including the philosophical tale *Candide* (1759), in which he spoofed the idea that ours is the "best of all possible worlds."

Voltaire was an adamant critic of religious intolerance and persecution. The memorable closing line of *Candide*, "Let us cultivate our garden," has been interpreted to mean that the proper course of action for humankind is to perform practical, useful work. Voltaire died in 1778 at the age of eighty-four, leaving behind a body of work that epitomizes the Enlightenment.

TABLE OF CONTENTS

The World of Voltaire and *Candide*
ix
—

Introduction by Gita May
xiii
—

CANDIDE
1
—

Endnotes
133
—

Inspired by *Candide*
139
—

Comments & Questions
141
—

For Further Reading
145
—

THE WORLD OF VOLTAIRE AND
CANDIDE

1694	Voltaire is born François-Marie Arouet in Paris on November 21.
1704	François enrolls at the Collège Louis-le-Grand, a Jesuit institution, where he studies classical literature and drama.
1711	After leaving Louis-le-Grand, François pursues writing as a career, despite his father's wishes that he study law.
1714	To the dismay of his father, François meets with members and explores the ideology of the radical Society of the Temple; he writes satirical poems.
1715	King Louis XIV dies. His great grandson, Louis XV, ascends to the throne, but because he is only five years old, the duke of Orleans assumes the regency until his death in 1723. The royal court leaves the confined environment of Versailles to take up residence in the more liberal atmosphere of Paris, one of the events that marks the beginning of the Enlightenment in France.
1717–1718	Beginning in May, François is imprisoned in the Bastille for eleven months after the duke of Orléans wrongly accuses him of writing two libelous poems about the French government. In prison, he writes his first dramatic tragedy, *Oedipe* (his version of the Oedipus myth) and *La Henriade*, an epic poem about Henry IV of France.
1718	The theatrical success of *Oedipe* wins François a pension from the regent.
1719	Francois-Marie Arouet assumes the pen name Voltaire.
1723	The first edition of *La Henriade* is published. Upon the

death of the duke of Orleans, Louis XV accedes to the throne. However, France is ruled by the duke of Bourbon and Cardinal de Fleury, who revamp France's economic policies.

1725   In September Voltaire attends Louis XV's marriage, at which three of his plays are performed.

1726   Voltaire is sent to the Bastille for the second time for challenging the chevalier de Rohan to a duel. After two weeks, he is offered exile as an alternative and emigrates to England, where he spends the next two and a half years learning English and studying the philosophies of philosopher John Locke and mathematician and physicist Isaac Newton. He also attends productions of the plays of William Shakespeare.

1728   The second edition of *La Henriade* is published.

1729   Voltaire gains the right to return to Paris.

1730   Indignant at the clergy's refusal to properly bury the body of famed actress Adrienne Lecouvreur, Voltaire writes a protest poem, *The Death of Mademoiselle Lecouvreur*. His tragedy *Brutus* receives accolades following its opening performance.

1731   Voltaire publishes the first of his historical works, *Charles XII*, a life of the Swedish monarch, which remains today a classic of biography.

1732   Voltaire's heroic tragedy *Zaire*, a tale of doomed love, is a success.

1733   Voltaire begins his long affair with Madame du Châtelet. *Letters Concerning the English Nation* is published in English. The book, which praises the English monarchy and the country's religious tolerance, is interpreted as critical of the French church and state.

1734   *Letters Concerning the English Nation* is published in French as *Lettres philosophiques*. It is banned in France, and Voltaire seeks refuge at Cirey in the province of Champagne, where for the next fifteen years he lives at the estate of Madame du Châtelet.

1735   Although granted the right to return to Paris, Voltaire chooses to remain at Cirey, returning to the city only occasionally. He spends time conducting physical and chemical experiments and writing. He begins a correspondence with Crown Prince Frederick of Prussia (later Frederick the Great), with whom he will have a rocky relationship.

1738   Eléments de la philosophie de Newton (Elements of Newton's Philosophy) is published.

1745   Through the influence of Madame de Pompadour, Louis XV's mistress, Voltaire is appointed the royal historiographer of France.

1746   He is elected to the prestigious French Academy.

1747   Voltaire's philosophical tale Zadig is published.

1749   Madame du Châtelet dies. Upon the invitation of Frederick the Great, Voltaire moves briefly to Potsdam.

1750   At Frederick's request, Voltaire goes to Berlin to serve as philosopher-poet at the royal court. He will stay for three years.

1751   While at the German court, Voltaire publishes the historical work Le siècle de Louis XIV (The Age of Louis XIV), which advocates for social and moral progress.

1752   Voltaire publishes Micromégas, a fantastic travelogue that reflects Newton's cosmology and Locke's empiricism, and attempts to fuse science and moral philosophy.

1753   Voltaire leaves Berlin after an argument with Frederick (the two will later reconcile and resume a correspondence). Unable to return to France, Voltaire stays in various towns on the border until December 1754, when he moves to Geneva.

1755   Voltaire purchases a villa, Les Délices, outside Geneva, and makes it his home. After a devastating earthquake kills tens of thousands in Lisbon, Voltaire rejects the concept of a rational and well-regulated universe, as advocated by the German philosopher Gottfried Wilhelm Leibniz.

1756   The Seven Years War begins and will last until 1763. It is fought in Europe, with North America, and India, by France, Austria, Russia, Saxony, Sweden, and eventually Spain one side, and Prussia, Great Britain, and

Hanover on the other. This complex war is based on colonial rivalry between France and England, and a struggle for power in Germany between Austria and Prussia. Along with the Lisbon earthquake, it deeply affects Voltaire's outlook. Voltaire publishes *Poème sur le désastre de Lisbonne* (*Poem on the Disaster of Lisbon*), in which he signals his rejection of Leibniz's approach.

1757   After its seventh volume is published, the *Encyclopédie*—co-edited by Denis Diderot to provide a survey of human knowledge from the standpoint of the Enlightenment (Voltaire was a contributor)—is banned in France.

1759   Voltaire buys an estate, Ferney, near the France-Switzerland border. It will become the intellectual capital of western Europe, and Voltaire will spend his last years there writing narratives, plays, and personal letters. The most notable of the narratives, published this year, is the philosophical tale *Candide*—an attack on the evils of religious fanaticism, war, colonialism, and slavery.

1764   The *Dictionnaire philosophique*—a compendium of Voltaire's thoughts on a variety of subjects—is published.

1774   Louis XV dies, and Louis XVI takes the throne.

1778   Voltaire returns to Paris, where he is welcomed by the public. On May 30 he dies there at age eighty-four. His body initially is buried on the grounds of an abbey in Champagne.

1791   Voltaire's remains are brought back to Paris and buried in the Panthéon.

1787–   The philosophy of the thinkers of the Enlightenment,
1799   including Voltaire—expressed in the motto "Liberty, Fraternity, Equality"—inspires the French Revolution. The subsequent reign of Napoleon Bonaparte preserves many of the freedoms won during the Revolution, including religious toleration and the abolition of serfdom. The Civil Code, also known as the Napoleonic Code, is established; it remains as the basis for the system of civil law in modern France.

INTRODUCTION

Voltaire would probably have been both pleasantly surprised as well as bemused by the exceptional and enduring popularity of *Candide*, which he viewed as one of his minor works, unworthy to vie with his tragedies, historical essays, and epic and philosophical poems, on which he staked his posthumous reputation.

On November 21, 1694, on the left bank of the Seine, in the heart of Paris, a sickly infant named François-Marie Arouet was born and not expected to live. Contrary to this inauspicious beginning, he would fool everyone (something he later excelled at doing) and take his final leave of life only in his eighty-fourth year. By then he had become the most illustrious author of his age under his chosen pen name of Voltaire; this name he adorned with the article *de*, a common practice among writers of bourgeois origin with aristocratic aspirations, before and even after the French Revolution, as Beaumarchais and Balzac could attest.

The father of young Arouet, François Arouet, was an ambitious and highly respected lawyer whose ancestors had been merchant drapers and who in 1683 had married Marie-Marguerite d'Aumard (also spelled Daumard), a member of the minor provincial mobility. Unlike Rousseau or Diderot, Voltaire evidenced no sentimental attachment to his family and little curiosity about his roots, childhood, and early formative years. If he took little interest in his ancestry, it was probably because he deemed it of no special historical or cultural significance. As for his immediate family members, he barely knew his mother, who died when he was ten, and he never seemed to have felt a nostalgic urge to romanticize her; and he did not get along with his strict, quick-tempered father, who in turn would strongly disapprove of his son's iconoclastic writings and highly controversial reputation. Voltaire was the least introspective of authors and still adhered to the classical notion that public self-revelation is not only in bad taste, it smacks of the obscene; in Pascal's words, "the self is hateful." There furthermore was a secretive facet to his complex nature, and he had his own reasons for not dwelling on or divulging details of his private life and family relationships.

At the age of ten young Arouet was placed at the renowned Jesuit College Louis-le-Grand, in the Latin Quarter, where he received a solid education in the classics, where his knowledgeable and supportive masters nurtured his precocious interest and talent in drama and poetry, and where he formed lifelong friendships with some of his classmates.

Having completed his studies in 1711, the seventeen-year-old Arouet adamantly refused to obey his father's stern injunction to go to law school, for by now he was intent on becoming a man of letters. While still at Louis-le-Grand, he had been introduced to a group of Epicurean libertines, or freethinkers who subsequently congregated at the Temple of the Knights of Malta and therefore became known as the Society of the Temple. He rubbed elbows with young aristocrats chafing under the austere and oppressively religiosity of the court of the aging Louis XIV, who would die in 1715, and his successor, the notorious Philippe II, duke of Orléans, regent of France until 1723. This period was marked in elite and sophisticated circles by a disdainful disregard for traditional values and a hedonistic love of life and of beauty in all its forms, especially in the arts and letters.

Young Arouet thrived in this pleasure-loving milieu, increasingly asserting himself as an aspiring dramatist, and author of light and satirical verses, a wit especially gifted with sharp, ironic repartees, and a skeptic in religious matters. In 1718 he had his first great success with his tragedy *Oedipe*, his version of the Oedipus myth made famous by Sophocles and also treated by Pierre Corneille, the great seventeenth-century French dramatist. The triumph of his play induced him in 1719 to leave his bourgeois origins behind once and for all by adopting the more euphonious and aristocratic pen name "de Voltaire."

Meanwhile, he had already gotten a rather bitter taste of Old Regime justice when, as the author of satirical verses directed against the regent, he was forced to spend eleven months in the infamous Bastille prison, from May 1717 to April 1718. Then in 1726 an incident occurred that would mark the turning point in his life and career. Voltaire quarreled with the chevalier de Rohan, scion of one of the most powerful French families, who had his lackeys beat him up for blatantly assuming an aristocratic name; the young writer failed to gather support among his aristocratic friends in his desperate attempts to find redress in a duel with the chevalier, who persistently refused to honor a mere commoner with this distinction. Instead he was once more hustled off to the Bastille, but after a two-week stay was offered the alternative of going into exile. He opted for England.

Voltaire's stay in England, from May 1726 to November 1728, profoundly transformed and enriched his intellectual and aesthetic outlook, as the Lettres philosophiques (1734), one of his most original and striking works, (an English version titled Letters Concerning the English Nation had appeared in 1733) amply testifies. He vividly and most sympathetically evokes life in eighteenth-century England, primarily in order to contrast it favorably with French laws, customs, traditions, science, philosophy, and even literature. He humorously describes the apparently bizarre mores of the Quakers, primarily in order to underscore religious intolerances in France. Also featured are such powerful political institutions as the English Parliament, with its House of Commons; English empiricist philosophy and science as embodied by Francis Bacon, John Locke, and Isaac Newton; and English tragedy and comedy, with the focus on William Shakespeare as a new kind of genius, untrammeled by classical rules and conventions. From a sharp-tongued wit, a gifted poet, and a dramatist, Voltaire had made himself over into a philosophe who soon would become the undisputed leader of the Enlightenment movement. The book on England was promptly condemned and publicly burned in France, and its author had to seek refuge near the eastern border, in the province of Champagne, at Cirey, where he settled in the château of Madame du Châtelet, a remarkable woman who was a brilliant intellectual and a scientist in her own right.

Voltaire lived in Cirey for fifteen happy and productive years, from 1734 until 1749, when the premature death of Madame du Châtelet left him disconsolate and at long last open to the repeated offers of hospitality of Fredrick the Great of Prussia, a long-time admirer and correspondent of the *philosophe*, who had been urging him to become his permanent guest at his court at Potsdam.

While at Cirey Voltaire deepened his knowledge of Newtonian mathematics and physics, which in 1738 would result in *Éléments de la philosophie de Newton (Elements of Newton's Philosophy)*, a distinguished work of scientific popularization. He also pondered the philosophy of Leibniz at the instigation of Madame du Châtelet, and he embarked upon his great cultural histories, most notably *Le siècle de Louis XIV (The Age of Louis XIV)*, published in 1751, in which he pointedly extols the glorious scientific, artistic, and literary achievements of France during the glorious reign of the so-called Sun King at the expense of Louis XV.

During his stay in England and at Cirey Voltaire's outlook on life was essentially optimistic. In the twenty-fifth and last of his *Lettres philosophiques* he sternly took Pascal to task for his pessimistic depiction of the human condition, describing him as a "sublime misanthrope"; and in his poem *Le Mondain* (The Worldly One), published in 1736, he sharply ridiculed the myth of primitive happiness and innocence during the so-called Golden Age, as embodied in the biblical story of Adam and Eve. Conversely, he extolled the Epicurean delights of comfort and luxury brought about by modern civilization. In spite of his controversial reputation, he garnered such high official honors as being elected to the French Academy in 1746. He was still convinced that, on the whole, Newton's eminently rational laws permitted human beings to accommodate themselves and seek their happiness within this orderly universe, set in motion by a supremely powerful but also benevolent being. And as a deist, he generally also subscribed to Gottfried Wilhelm Leibniz's theory that God would not create a universe other than the best of all possible universes, as expounded in his *Theodicy* (1710).

Voltaire's stay at the court of Frederick II, from 1750 until 1753, turned out to be an unmitigated disaster. Frederick was basically an autocrat, in spite of his much-publicized image as an enlightened "philosopher king." Voltaire's irrepressible wit and bold irreverence were bound to displease and eventually anger his royal host, and eventually Voltaire had to leave Prussia hurriedly and under humiliating circumstances. After some hesitation as to where to find a safe refuge, he settled down in Geneva in December 1759, when he moved to a property he acquired at nearby Ferney, which would be his retreat for the next nineteen years, until shortly before his death in Paris, on May 30, 1778.

Voltaire's early optimism underwent a profound change under the impact of events in his personal life as well as in reaction to those natural and man-made catastrophes that made him keenly aware of human suffering and misery, not to mention the multiple dangers that constantly threaten our very existence, let alone our well-being and chances of achieving happiness. His own disappointments—notably the unexpected loss of Madame du Châtelet, the unrelenting hostility of the court of Louis XV, the disenchantment with Frederick, and the precariousness of his personal situation—were compounded by his intense and immediate empathy; he spontaneously identified with all victims of calamities, war, injustice, prejudice, and intolerance.

The news of the terrible Lisbon earthquake of November 1, 1755, which claimed tens of thousands of lives, overwhelmed him with dreadful images of women and children buried under the rubble, and inspired his eloquently anguished *Poème sur le désastre de Lisbonne* (Poem on the Disaster of Lisbon), published in 1756, in which he clearly signals his rejection of Leibniz's concept of a rational and well-regulated universe. The protracted and devastating Seven Years War (1756–1763), which began when Frederick invaded Saxony and soon expanded the lingering hostilities between France and England into a European conflagration, also deeply affected Voltaire's outlook on the human condition.

Voltaire began writing philosophical *contes* (tales) relatively late in his career and almost as an afterthought, for he subscribed to the neoclassical canon and hierarchy of literary genres according to which tragedy in verse and epic poetry gave an author his most reliable passport to posterity and immortality. Novels, short stories, and *contes* were looked upon suspiciously as upstart genres with no credible aesthetic or even moral pedigree.

Voltaire began with the traditional short story or novella, and transformed it into the *conte philosophique*, or philosophical tale, a fast-moving and highly entertaining story combining multiple adventures and voyages with an underlying philosophical and moral theme, written in a pithy style replete with humor, satire, irony, and sly sexual innuendoes. Indeed, ridicule would be Voltaire's most effective weapon against his main targets: fanaticism, intolerance, war, and cruelty.

One of Voltaire's early philosophical tales is *Zadig*, subtitled *La Destinée* (Destiny), which appeared in 1747. It is set in the kind of whimsically imaginary and exotic Oriental setting dear to eighteenth-century authors from Montesquieu to Diderot. The uncannily wise, resourceful, and resilient Zadig, whose name derives from the Arabic *sadik* ("just"), undergoes a number of trials and tribulations, and when faced with disconcerting instances of injustice and suffering, and with the unpredictability and apparent randomness of life in general, anxiously questions and even objects to the notion of a world regulated by a benevolent Providence. But Zadig eventually overcomes adversity and reluctantly submits to the reassuring belief that Providence works in mysterious and unfathomable ways for the ultimately greater good of humanity.

While still in Prussia, Voltaire published *Micromégas* in 1752. Partially inspired by Swift's *Gulliver's Travels* (1726) and by Cyrano de Bergerac's two fantastic romances about visits to the moon and sun——*Autre Monde: ou, Les Estats et empires de la lune* (1657) and *Les Estats et empires du soleil* (1662)——it is a science-fiction story of fantastic, humorous interplanetary travel that strongly reflects Newton's cosmology and Locke's empiricism, and that pointedly resorts to fictional and comic devices in order to fuse science and moral philosophy. In a universe of multiple planets inhabited by creatures of various gigantic dimensions, the remarkable scientific knowledge of the minuscule earthlings is duly acknowledged, but at the same time their basic ignorance in matters of ultimate human values, masked by hubris and pedantry, is pointedly ridiculed and excoriated, especially when viewed from the perspective of two extraterrestrial visitors, Micromégas, the giant originating from Sirius, and his smaller but still huge traveling companion, whom he had picked up on the planet Saturn in the course of his celestial peregrinations.

Candide, the hero of the philosophical tale by that name, came into the world in January 1759 unacknowledged by his creator. The work was proposed as a translation "from the German of Doctor Ralph, with the additions found in the Doctor's pocket when he died at Minden, in the Year of Our Lord 1759." It was customary for Voltaire to deny the paternity of his most potentially controversial writings by mischievously attributing them to imaginary or even real persons to maintain a near total silence about the circumstances and composition of his works of prose fiction.

Voltaire was hardly an introspective author, and in this, as in so many other respects, he stands at the opposite pole from Jean-Jacques Rousseau, who insisted, in full knowledge of the dangers involved, on publicly proclaiming the authorship of all his writings and who in both his Confessions (1781, 1788) and correspondence provides much detailed information on their genesis, publication, and immediate public response, as well as official reaction.

Another explanation for Voltaire's reticence about his philosophical tales is his understandable if mistaken belief that these were relatively inconsequential productions belonging to the much decried and maligned genre of the novel, and that they would not fare well with future readers, especially when considered alongside his far more ambitious and serious works—his tragedies, epic and philosophical poems, and historical essays. Whatever Voltaire's own motives or thinking about Candide may have been, there is a persistent but erroneous legend that he dashed off by dictation the thirty chapters of the tale in three days. It is of course far more likely that he wrote Candide over a ten-month period in 1758 and completed the manuscript, with final revisions and additions, in the fall of that year.

The slender book first came off the presses of the brothers Cramer, publishers in Geneva, in January 1759. It was promptly disseminated and repeatedly republished in Paris and elsewhere. Even though it was swiftly condemned by both French and Swiss authorities, and copies were seized in printing shops in Paris and Geneva, it sold briskly under the counters. No official effort to suppress Candide could prevent it from becoming one of the most sensational forbidden best-sellers of pre-Revolutionary France and indeed Eu-

rope. Within a year, there were at least three English translations
and one edition in Italian.

In 1758 the sixty-four-year-old Voltaire had personally experienced an unusually vast range of human situations and emotions,
and he had become keenly aware of the existence of evil, unhap-
piness, and injustice in this world. He had also come to the reali-
zation that there were no satisfactory theological or philosophical
explanations to justify or account for the horrors that so persistently
dog humankind.

He had acquired an enormous intellectual and multicultural frame
of reference thanks to his unquenchable intellectual curiosity,
through his omnivorous reading, and especially through his extensive research for his historical works and philosophical essays. He
was now at the height of his powers and in full possession of his
craft as a writer who over the decades had tirelessly practiced, per-
fected, and mastered all the literary genres and rhetorical techniques
and devices.

The reasons for Candide's immediate and enduring success with
readers are many. It is a supremely wrought tragicomedy that slyly
and irresistibly induces us to laugh at and simultaneously reflect
upon the most dreadful events that befall humankind. It appeals to
us today because, nearly 250 years after its publication, it has lost
none of its relevance or satirical sting. It is particularly modern and
pertinent because its dark cosmic vision is essentially in keeping
with our own awareness of what separates our need for order, clar-
ity, and rationality from the brutal reality of a chaotic world.

The fiercely relentless attack Candide unleashes against the evils of
religious fanaticism, war, colonialism, slavery, and mass atrocities
is more relevant than ever. The naïve, young hero of the tale obstinately seeks personal happiness in a world beleaguered by all
kinds of catastrophes wrought by the blind, unleashed forces of
nature—such as earthquakes and epidemic diseases—as well as by
violent, destructive human passions.

The tale opens with a kind of idyll that revisits in a parodic and
rococo mode themes originally brought to life in the Garden of
Eden. The castle in Westphalia, which belongs to the proud baron
of Thunder-ten-tronckh, and its incongruous inhabitants are for the
gentle and innocent Candide a paradise from which he is suddenly

and brutally expelled when he is caught kissing Cunégonde, the baron's daughter, a pleasingly plump, wholesome, and docile young woman.

A gentle, honest, and appealingly naïve young man, reputed to be the illegitimate offspring of the sister of the baron Thunder-ten-tronckh and an honorable nobleman whom she refused to marry because of his insufficiently ancient lineage, Candide is the eager and wide-eyed disciple of his pedantic tutor Pangloss, who relentlessly lectures to him on "metaphysico-theologo-cosmolonigology," a comic formula of Voltaire's invention meant to ridicule Leibniz's philosophical optimism.

Throughout the dreadful catastrophes that will befall Candide, Pangloss, and their companions in misery, Pangloss will obstinately and blindly stick to his unshakable belief that "this is the best of all possible worlds."

Upon being summarily kicked out of the baron's castle, Candide is immediately plunged into an incomprehensible and unpredictable world ruled by overwhelmingly powerful and evil forces, both natural and human. Forcibly impressed into the army of the king of the Bulgars, he witnesses all the horrors of war in a fierce battle between the Bulgars and the Abares from which he barely escapes with his life. While the kings of the two opposing armies were having solemn "Te Deums" sung, each of his own camp, Candide fled this "heroic butchery" that left behind not only heaps of dead and dying soldiers on the battlefield, but also surrounding villages in ashes, their inhabitants savagely massacred. Candide is befriended by James the Anabaptist, and also unexpectedly meets Dr. Pangloss, by now reduced to the pitiful state of a beggar grossly disfigured by syphilis. This motley group starts for Lisbon, and their ship is wrecked in a terrible storm off the coast of Portugal. James is drowned, while Candide and Pangloss barely manage to reach the shore of Portugal just as an earthquake shakes its capital, crushing 30,000 inhabitants under the ruins and engulfing what is left of the city in the flames and ashes of terrible fires.

In order to punish those judged wicked enough to have caused this disaster and to prevent other earthquakes from occurring, the rulers of Lisbon treat the people to the spectacle of a splendid *auto-da-fé*. While Pangloss is hanged, Candide is whipped to within an inch of his life. A charitable old woman takes care of him and leads him to Cunégonde; the damsel had barely survived being raped and stabbed in her father's castle, and has since become the mistress of Don Issachar, who is a Jew, and the Grand Inquisitor, both of whom Candide finds himself obliged to kill as threatening rivals when they discover him in a compromising situation with the young woman. As a result, the lovers, accompanied by the old woman, flee to Cadiz, where they embark for Paraguay. During the lengthy sea voyage, the old woman, who happens to be the daughter of Pope Urban X and the Princess of Palestrina, relates her own sad story, filled with multiple bloody adventures and calamities in the course of which she was raped, sold into slavery, stricken with the plague, had one of her buttocks cut off, was sent to Russia where she fell to the lot of a boyard who gave her twenty lashes per day, and ended up becoming a servant of Don Issachar and assigned to Cunégonde.

After the ship lands in Buenos Aires, our passengers are the guests of the Governor, who promptly develops a mad and jealous infatuation with Cunégonde. Once more, Candide has to leave behind his beloved and flee for his life, this time in the company of Cacambo, a recently acquired valet, part Spanish and part South American Indian, who had himself acquired a rich and variegated experience of life. Arriving in Paraguay, Candide meets the Commandant of the Jesuits, who turns out to be Cunégonde's brother; he has also somehow survived the massacre in his father's castle and has since become a Jesuit priest and a colonel in the King of Spain's troops. However, upon learning of Candide's intention of marrying his sister, he becomes enraged and draws his sword, and in the ensuing violent fight Candide has to stab him in self-defense.

Believing he has killed Cunégonde's brother, Candide (with Cacambo in tow) promptly takes to the road again, rescues two young girls amorously pursued by monkeys, and is captured by the Oreillons, a tribe of cannibalistic Indians with a special liking for Jesuit flesh; the two are freed when the resourceful Cacambo persuades the Indians that his master, far from being a Jesuit, has just killed one. Pursuing their journey, Candide and Cacambo painfully reach the isolated country of El Dorado, surrounded by nearly impassable mountains and precipices, and find themselves in a utopian society that, as an enlightened monarchy, offers its subjects the abundant fruits of its natural riches, as well as peace, prosperity, liberty, tolerance, and justice. After two months in this happy retreat, Candide becomes restless and decides to resume his travels and his quest for his beloved Cunégonde. He and Cacambo set out with a hundred sheep, plentiful provision, and huge amounts of gold, diamond, and other precious stones. However, after a hundred days of strenuous travel, only two sheep survive. In Surinam, a Dutch colony, they encounter an African slave missing his left leg and right hand, the result of the barbaric treatment he has incurred while working in the sugar mills of his master. "It is at this cost that you eat sugar in Europe," is his sad comment.

Trying in vain to rejoin Cunégonde, the too-trusting Candide is promptly swindled out of most of his possessions. In order to have a better chance at rescuing Cunégonde, Candide sends the more worldy-wise Cacambo to Buenos Aires and he plans to await them in Venice. He sets sail for Bordeaux in the hope of reaching his destination by way of Paris, after having selected as a traveling companion an impoverished scholar named Martin, who has also been the victim of many misfortunes and who, as a Manichaeist, is the pessimistic counterpart of Pangloss. In Paris, Candide is introduced into high society, with its fine suppers, slanderous gossip, and gambling at cards. Arrested as a suspicious foreigner, he buys his freedom with some of his diamonds from El Dorado and is shipped off to Portsmouth, England, where he witnesses the summary execution of Admiral Byng. From Portsmouth, Candide proceeds to Venice, where he encounters Paquette, Cunégonde's maid, and Cacambo, who informs him that Cunégonde is in Constantinople. In Venice, he is the guest of Senator Pococuranté, a wealthy Venetian nobleman whose social privileges and riches have made him a complete disbeliever in the ultimate value of all cultural and literary achievements.

In the Venetian galley that carries Candide to Constantinople, where he hopes to reunite with his beloved Cunégonde, Candide unexpectedly finds Pangloss and Cunégonde's brother among the galley slaves. He is informed that Pangloss survived his hanging in Lisbon because of a bungled knot and that Cunégonde's brother survived his wound, which had not been fatal after all. When Candide and his companions arrive in Constantinople, they buy Cunégonde and the old woman from their masters. By then, however, Cunégonde has lost her good looks, but Candide feels he cannot go back on his word, while her brother obstinately persists in his objections, which can only be overcome by having him sent back to complete his stint as a galley slave.

Upon arriving in Constantinople, Candide purchases a little farm, but after having survived so many disasters the little group cannot at first easily settle into a calm, uneventful existence. Pangloss still tries to lecture his erstwhile disciple, but the latter interrupts the learned doctor with the simple, pragmatic, and ultimately hopeful observation that "we must cultivate our garden." In other words, life is made bearable by useful activity rather than by idle theorizing.

To summarize the plot of *Candide* is of course to leave out what makes it one of the great masterpieces of satirical and comical literature. It is a fast-paced adventure story and travelogue, an unsentimental love story, a fantasy replete with history. Comic effects are generally achieved by the staccato rhythm of the narration, by the jarring contrast between the dramatic content and the coolly dispassionate style, and by the absence of any psychological depth for the major characters of the tale, which makes them like marionettes, manipulated at will by their creator.

While it is a ferocious attack on philosophical optimism, *Candide* is not a pessimistic work, for it proclaims the human capacity to survive the worst calamities and to endure and even prosper in a world replete with war, cruelty, misery, persecution, and religious intolerance.

Gita May is Professor of French at Columbia University. She has published extensively on the French Enlightenment, eighteenth-century aesthetics, Diderot and Rousseau, literature and the arts, the novel and autobiography, the revolutionary and post-revolutionary era, and women in literature, history, and the arts. She is the author of *Diderot et Baudelaire, critiques d'art* (1957, second ed. 1967), *De Jean-Jacques Rousseau à Madame Roland* (1964), *Madame Roland and the Age of Revolution* (winner of the Van Amringe Distinguished Book Award; 1970), *Stendhal and the Age of Napoléon* (1977), extensive monographs on Julie de Lespinasse (1991), Elisabeth Vigée Le Brun (1994), Germaine de Staël (1995), George Sand (1994), Rebecca West (1996), and Anita Brookner (1997), and numerous articles, contributions to collections of essays, and book reviews and review articles. She was honored by the American Society for Eighteenth-Century Studies as one of the Society's "Great Teachers."

CANDIDE,
OR OPTIMISM

CONTENTS

CHAPTER I

How Candide was brought up in a magnificent castle;
and how he was driven out of it

11

———

CHAPTER II

What happened to Candide among the Bulgarians

14

———

CHAPTER III

How Candide escaped from the Bulgarians, and what happened
to him afterwards

17

———

CHAPTER IV

How Candide found his old Master Pangloss again,
and what happened to them

20

———

CHAPTER V

A Tempest, a Shipwreck, an Earthquake, and what else happened to Dr.
Pangloss, Candide, and James the Anabaptist

25

———

CHAPTER VI

How the Portuguese made a superb auto-da-fé to prevent any future
Earthquakes, and how Candide was publicly whipped

28

———

CHAPTER VII

How the Old Woman took care of Candide, and how he found
the Object of his Love

30

———

CHAPTER VIII

The History of Cunégonde

33

———

CHAPTER IX

What happened to Cunégonde, Candide, the Grand Inquisitor, and the Jew

36

———

CHAPTER X

In what distress Candide, Cunégonde, and the Old Woman arrived at
Cadiz; and of their Embarkation

39

———

CHAPTER XI

The History of the Old Woman

41

———

CHAPTER XII

The Adventures of the Old Woman (continued)

46

———

CHAPTER XIII
How Candide was obliged to leave the fair Cunégonde
and the Old Woman
51
———

CHAPTER XIV
How Candide and Cacambo were received by the Jesuits in Paraguay
54
———

CHAPTER XV
How Candide killed the Brother of his dear Cunégonde
59
———

CHAPTER XVI
What happened to our two Travellers with two Girls, two Monkeys, and
the savages called Oreillons
61
———

CHAPTER XVII
Candide and his Valet arrive in the Country of El Dorado.
What they saw there
66
———

CHAPTER XVIII
What they saw in the Country of El Dorado
70
———

CHAPTER XIX
What happened to them at Surinam, and how Candide got to know Martin
76
———

CHAPTER XX
What happened to Candide and Martin at sea
81
———

CHAPTER XXI
Candide and Martin draw near to the coast of France. They reason with each other
84
———

CHAPTER XXII
What happened to Candide and Martin in France
86
———

CHAPTER XXIII
Candide and Martin touch upon the English Coast; what they see there
99
———

CHAPTER XXIV
About Pacquette and Friar Giroflée
101
———

CHAPTER XXV
Candide and Martin pay a visit to Signor Pococuranté, a noble Venetian
106
———

CHAPTER XXVI

Candide and Martin sup with six strangers; and who they were

112

———

CHAPTER XXVII

Candide's Voyage to Constantinople

116

———

CHAPTER XXVIII

What happened to Candide, Cunégonde, Pangloss, Martin, etc.

120

———

CHAPTER XXIX

*In what manner Candide found Miss Cunégonde
and the Old Woman again*

124

———

CHAPTER XXX

Conclusion

126

———

LIST OF PENCIL PLATES

DR. PANGLOSS SURVEYS THE WORLD
Frontispiece
—

THE BULGARS LEAVING THUNDER-
TEN-TRONCKH CASTLE
22
—

THE RETURN OF DON ISSACHAR
37
—

THE TOILET OF THE POPE'S DAUGHTER
42
—

THE RESCUE OF THE BARON
58
—

AN OREILLON RECEPTION
64
—

THE ILLNESS OF CANDIDE IN PARIS
89
—

THE CRUCIAL INCISION
122

I

How Candide was brought up in a magnificent castle; and how he was driven out of it

In the country of Westphalia,* in the castle of the most noble baron of Thunder-ten-tronckh, lived a youth whom nature had endowed with a most sweet disposition. His face was the true index of his mind. He had a solid judgment joined to the most unaffected simplicity; and hence, I presume, he had his name of Candide. The old servants of the house suspected him to have been the son of the baron's sister by a very good sort of a gentleman of the neighbourhood, whom that young lady refused to marry, because he could produce no more than seventy-one quarterings† in his arms, the rest of the genealogical tree belonging to the family having been lost through the injuries of time.

The baron was one of the most powerful lords in Westphalia, for his castle had not only a gate, but even windows, and his great hall was hung with tapestry. He used to hunt with his mastiffs and spaniels instead of greyhounds; his groom served him for huntsman, and the parson of the parish officiated as his grand almoner. He was called "My Lord" by all his people, and everyone laughed at his stories.

My Lady Baroness weighed three hundred and fifty pounds, and consequently was a person of no small consideration; and she did the honours of the house with a dignity that commanded universal respect. Her daughter, Cunégonde, was about seventeen years of age, fresh-coloured, comely, plump and amiable. The baron's son seemed to be a youth in every respect worthy of his father. Pangloss,‡ the tutor, was the oracle of the family, and little Candide

---

*Province in western Germany.
†Genealogical divisions on a coat of arms indicating degrees of nobility.
‡All tongue (Greek).

listened to his instructions with all the simplicity natural to his age and disposition.

Master Pangloss taught the metaphysico-theologo-cosmolonigology.* He could prove admirably that there is no effect without a cause, and in this best of all possible worlds the baron's castle was the most magnificent of all castles, and my lady the best of all possible baronesses.

"It is demonstrable," said he, "that things cannot be otherwise than they are; for as all things have been created for some end, they must necessarily be created for the best end. Observe, for instance, the nose is formed for spectacles; therefore we wear spectacles. The legs are visibly designed for stockings; accordingly we wear stockings. Stones were made to be hewn and to construct castles; therefore my lord has a magnificent castle; for the greatest baron in the province ought to be the best lodged. Swine were intended to be eaten; therefore we eat pork all year round. And they who assert that everything is right, do not express themselves correctly; they should say that everything is best."[1]

Candide listened attentively, and believed implicitly; for he thought Miss Cunégonde excessively handsome though he never had the courage to tell her so. He concluded that after the happiness of being Baron of Thunder-ten-tronckh, the next was that of being Miss Cunégonde, the next that of seeing her every day, and the last that of hearing the doctrine of Master Pangloss, the greatest philosopher of the whole province, and consequently of the whole world.

One day when Miss Cunégonde went to take a walk in the little neighbouring woods, which was called a park, she saw through the bushes the sage Dr. Pangloss giving a lecture in experimental philosophy to her mother's chambermaid, a little brown wench, very pretty and very tractable. As Miss Cunégonde had a natural disposition toward the sciences, she observed with the utmost attention the experiments which were repeated before her eyes; she perfectly well understood the force of the doctor's reasoning upon causes and effects. She returned home greatly flurried, quite pensive and filled

---

* "Cosmolo" indicates "cosmology," a term invented by Christian Wolff, disciple of Leibniz; "nigo" calls to mind "nincompoop" in French.

with the desire of knowledge, imagining that she might be a sufficing reason for young Candide, and he for her.

On her way back she happened to meet Candide. She blushed;
he blushed also. She wished him a good morning in a flattering
tone; he returned the salute without knowing what he said. The
next day, as they were rising from the dinner table, Cunégonde and
Candide slipped behind a screen; Miss dropped her handkerchief;
the young man picked it up. She innocently took hold of his hand,
and he as innocently kissed hers with a warmth, a sensibility, a
grace—all very particular: their lips met; their eyes sparkled; their
knees trembled; their hands strayed. The baron chanced to come
by; he took note of the cause and effect, and without hesitation
saluted Candide with some notable kicks on the rear, and drove him
out of the castle. Miss Cunégonde, the tender, the lovely Miss Cunégonde, fainted away, and, as soon as she came to herself, the
baroness boxed her ears. Thus a general consternation was spread
over this most magnificent and most agreeable of all possible castles.

II

What happened to Candide among the Bulgarians[2]

C andide, driven out of this earthly paradise, wandered a long time without knowing where he went; sometimes he raised his eyes, all wet with tears, towards heaven, and sometimes he cast a melancholy look towards the magnificent castle, where the fairest of young baronesses lived. He laid himself down to sleep in a furrow, heart-broken, and supperless. The snow fell in great flakes and in the morning, when he awoke, he was almost frozen to death; however, he dragged himself to the next town, which was called Walds-berghoff-trarbk-dikdorff, without a penny in his pocket, and half dead with hunger and fatigue. He took up his stand at the door of an inn. He had not been long there, before two men dressed in blue* fixed their eyes steadfastly upon him. "Faith, comrade," said one of them to the other, "there is a well-made young fellow, and of the right size"; upon which they approached Candide, and with the greatest civility and politeness invited him to dine with them. "Gentlemen," replied Candide, with a most engaging modesty, "you do me much honour; but I really don't have enough money to pay my share." "Money, sir," said one of the blues to him, "young persons of your appearance and merit never pay anything; why, are not you five feet five inches tall?" "Yes, gentlemen, that is really my size," replied he, with a low bow. "Come then, sir, sit down with us; we will not only pay your bill, but we will never allow such a clever young fellow as you to be short on money. Mankind were born to assist one another." "You are perfectly right, gentlemen," said Candide, "this is precisely the doctrine of Master Pangloss; and I am convinced that everything is for the best." His

---

*Frederick the Great's recruiting officers wore blue uniforms.

generous companions next begged him to accept a few crowns,
which he readily complied with, at the same time offering them an
I.O.U. for the payment, which they refused, and then sat down at
the table together. "Have you not a great affection for——?" "O
yes; I have a great affection for the lovely Miss Cunégonde." "Maybe
so," replied one of the blues; "but that is not the question. We are
asking you whether you have not a great affection for the King of
the Bulgarians?" "For the King of the Bulgarians?" said Candide.
"Oh, Lord! not at all; why, I never saw him in my life." "Is it
possible! Oh, he is a most charming king. Come, we must drink his
health." "With all my heart, gentlemen," says Candide, and he
drinks his glass. "That will do!" cry the blues; "you are now the
support, the defender, the hero of the Bulgarians; your fortune is
made; your future is assured." So saying, they handcuff him, and
carry him away to the regiment. There he is made to wheel about
to the right, to the left, to draw his rammer, to return his rammer,
to present, to fire, to march; and they give him thirty blows with
a cane. The next day he performs his exercise a little better, and
they give him but twenty. The day after he comes off with ten, and
is looked upon as a young fellow of surprising genius by all his
comrades.

Candide was struck with amazement and really could not conceive how he came to be a hero. One fine spring morning he took
it into his head to take a walk, and he marched straight forward,
conceiving it to be a privilege of the human species, as well as of
animals in general, to make use of their legs how and when they
pleased. He had not gone above two leagues when he was overtaken
by four other heroes, six feet high, who bound him neck and heels
and carried him to a dungeon. At the court-martial, he was asked
which he preferred: to be flogged thirty-six times by the whole
regiment, or to have his brains blown out with a dozen musket
balls. In vain did he remonstrate with them, that the human will is
free, and that he chose neither. They pressed him to make a choice,
and he determined, in virtue of that divine gift called free-will, to
be flogged thirty-six times. He had gone through two floggings,
and the regiment being composed of 2,000 men, that made for him
exactly 4,000 strokes, which lay bare all his muscles and nerves
from the nape of his neck to his rump. As they were preparing to

make him set out the third time our young hero, unable to support
it any longer, begged as a favour they would be so obliging as to
shoot him through the head. The favour being granted, a bandage
was tied over his eyes, and he was made to kneel down. At that
very instant the King of the Bulgars, happening to pass by, made a
stop and enquired into the delinquent's crime, and being a prince
of great genius, he found, from what he heard of Candide, that he
was a young metaphysician, entirely ignorant of the world; and
therefore, out of his great clemency, he condescended to pardon
him, for which his name will be celebrated in every journal and in
every age. A skilful surgeon cured the flagellated Candide in three
weeks, by means of emollient unguents prescribed by Dioscorides.*
His sores were now skinned over, and he was able to march, when
the King of the Bulgarians gave battle to the King of the Abares.[3]

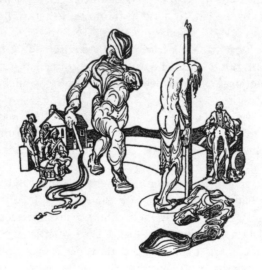

---

*Greek physician of the first century A.D who traveled with the Roman army as a
surgeon and wrote a treatise on medical remedies.

III

How Candide escaped from the Bulgarians, and what happened to him afterwards

Never was anything so gallant, so well accoutred, so brilliant, and so finely disposed as the two armies. The trumpets, fifes, oboes, drums and cannon made such harmony as never was heard in hell itself. The entertainment began by a discharge of the cannon, which in the twinkling of an eye lay flat about 6,000 men on each side. The musket balls swept away, out of the best of all possible worlds, nine or ten thousand scoundrels that infected its surface. The bayonet was next the *sufficient reason** of the deaths of several thousands more. The whole might amount to 30,000 souls. Candide trembled like a philosopher, and concealed himself as well as he could during this heroic butchery.

At length, while the two kings were causing "Te Deum"† to be sung in each of their camps, Candide decided to go and reason somewhere else upon causes and effects. After passing over heaps of dead or dying men, the first place he came to was a neighbouring village in the Abarian territories which had been burnt to the ground by the Bulgarians, in accordance with the laws of war. Here lay a number of old men covered with wounds, who beheld their wives dying with their throats cut, and hugging their children to their breasts, all stained with blood. There several young virgins whose bodies had been ripped open, after they had satisfied the natural necessities of the Bulgarian heroes, breathed their last; while others, half burnt in the flames, begged to be despatched out of the world. The ground about them was covered with the brains, arms and legs of dead men.

---

*Phrase employed to ridicule the Leibnizian terminology of deterministic optimism.
†Satirical reference to the custom of warring nations to invoke the blessing of the Almighty and to ask Him for victory.

Candide made haste to another village, which belonged to the Bulgarians, and there he found that the heroic Abares had enacted the same tragedy. From there, continuing to walk over palpitating limbs, or through ruined buildings, at length he arrived beyond the theatre of war, with a little provision in his budget and Miss Cunégonde's image in his heart. When he arrived in Holland, his provisions ran out; but having heard that the inhabitants of that country were all rich and Christians, he made himself sure of being treated by them in the same manner as at the baron's castle, before he had been driven from there through the power of Miss Cunégonde's bright eyes.

He asked charity of several grave-looking people, who one and all answered him, that if he continued to beg, they would have him sent to the house of correction, where he would be taught to earn his bread.

He next addressed himself to a person* who was just come from haranguing a numerous assembly for a whole hour on the subject of charity. The orator, squinting at him under his broad-brimmed hat, asked him sternly what brought him there, and whether he was for the good cause? "Sir," said Candide in a submissive manner, "I conceive there can be no effect without a cause; everything is necessarily concatenated and arranged for the best. It was necessary that I should be banished from the presence of Miss Cunégonde; that I should afterwards be flogged; and it is necessary that I should beg for my bread, till I am able to get it: all this could not have been otherwise." "Hark ye, friend," said the orator, "do you think the Pope is Antichrist?" "Truly, I never heard anything about it," said Candide; "but whether he is or not I am in want of something to eat." "Thou deservest not to eat or to drink," replied the orator, "wretch, monster that you are! Away with you! Out of my sight, never come near me again as long as you live." The orator's wife happened to put her head out of the window at that instant, when, seeing a man who doubted whether the Pope was Antichrist, she emptied on his head a chamber-pot full of——. Good heavens! to what excess does religious zeal transport the female kind.

---

*What follows makes clear that this is a Protestant minister who is fanatical in his hatred of the Catholic religion.

A man who had never been christened, an honest Anabaptist*
named James, was witness to the cruel and ignominious treatment
inflicted on one of his brethren, to a rational, two-footed, unfledged
being.† Moved with pity, he carried Candide to his own house,
washed him, gave him meat and drink, and presented him with two
florins, at the same time proposing to instruct him in his own trade
of weaving Persian silks, which are manufactured in Holland. Candide, moved by so much goodness, threw himself at his feet, crying:
"Now I am convinced that my master Pangloss told me truth when
he said that everything was for the best in this world; for I am
infinitely more touched by your extraordinary generosity than with
the inhumanity of that gentleman in the black coat, and his wife."
The next day, as Candide was walking out, he met a beggar all
covered with scabs, his eyes were sunk in his head, the end of his
nose eaten off, his mouth drawn on one side, his teeth as black as
a cloak, snuffling and coughing most violently, and every time he
attempted to spit, out dropped a tooth.

---

*Christian sect that opposed infant baptism in favor of baptism on confession of
faith; in Holland, the Anabaptists were granted religious tolerance and refuge against
persecution.
†Refers to Aristotle's definition of man as a featherless biped.

IV

How Candide found his old Master Pangloss again, and what happened to them

Candide, divided between compassion and horror, but giving way to the former, bestowed on this shocking figure the two florins which the honest Anabaptist James had just before given to him. The spectre looked at him very earnestly, shed tears and threw his arms about his neck. Candide started back aghast. "Alas!" said the one wretch to the other, "don't you know your dear Pangloss?" "What are you saying? Is it you, my dear master—you I behold in this piteous plight? What dreadful misfortune has befallen you? What has made you leave the most magnificent and delightful of all castles? What has become of Miss Cunégonde, the mirror of young ladies, and Nature's masterpiece?" "Oh, Lord!" cried Pangloss, "I am so weak I cannot stand"; upon which Candide instantly led him to the Anabaptist's stable, and found him something to eat. As soon as Pangloss had refreshed himself a little Candide began to repeat his inquiries concerning Miss Cunégonde. "She is dead," replied the other. "Dead!" cried Candide, and immediately fainted. His friend recovered him by the help of a little bad vinegar, which he found by chance in the stable. Candide opened his eyes, and again repeated: "Dead! Is Miss Cunégonde dead? Ah, what has become of the best of worlds now? But how did she die? Was it for grief upon seeing her father kick me out of his magnificent castle?" "No," replied Pangloss. "Her body was ripped open by the Bulgarian soldiers after they had ravished her as much as it was possible for damsel to be ravished. They smashed her father's head for attempting to defend her; my lady her mother was cut in pieces; my poor pupil was served just in the same manner as his sister; and as for the castle they have not left one stone upon another. They have destroyed all the ducks and the sheep, the barns and the trees;

we have had our revenge, for the Abares have done the very same thing in a neighbouring barony, which belonged to a Bulgarian lord."

At hearing this, Candide fainted a second time, but, having come to himself again, he said all that was appropriate to the occasion. He asked about the cause and effect, as well as about the *sufficing reason*, that had reduced Pangloss to so miserable a condition. "Alas," replied the tutor, "it was love; love, the comfort of the human species; love, the preserver of the universe, the soul of all sensible beings; love, tender love!" "Alas," replied Candide, "I have had some knowledge of love myself, this sovereign of hearts, this soul of souls; yet it never cost me more than a kiss and twenty kicks in the rear. But how could this beautiful cause produce in you so hideous an effect?"

Pangloss replied as follows: "Oh, my dear Candide, you must remember Pacquette, that pretty wench who waited on our noble baroness; in her arms I tasted the pleasures of paradise, which produced these hell-torments with which you see me devoured. She was infected with disease,* and perhaps is since dead of it. She received this present of a learned cordelier, who traced it back to its source. He was indebted for it to an old countess, who caught it from a captain of cavalry, who caught it from a marchioness, who caught it from a page, the page received it from a Jesuit, who during his noviciate got it directly from one of the fellow adventurers of Christopher Columbus. For my part, I shall give it to nobody. I am a dying man."

"O sage Pangloss," cried Candide, "what a strange genealogy is this. Is not the devil at the root of it?" "Not at all," replied the great man; "it was a thing unavoidable, a necessary ingredient in the best of worlds; for if Columbus had not caught in an island in America this disease, which is evidently opposite to the great end of nature, we should have had neither chocolate nor cochineal.† It is also to be observed that, even to the present time, in this continent of ours,

---

*Syphilis.
†Scarlet dye made from the dried bodies of female cochineal (small, red, cactus-feeding) insects; imported from Mexico and Peru.

THE BULGARS LEAVING THUNDER-TEN-TRONCKH CASTLE.

this malady, like our religious controversies, has been confined to us. The Turks, the Indians, the Persians, the Chinese, the Siamese, and the Japanese are entirely unacquainted with it; but there is a *sufficing reason* for them to know it in a few centuries. In the meantime it is creating prodigious havoc among us, especially in those armies composed of well-disciplined hirelings,* who determine the fate of nations; for we may safely affirm that, when an army of 30,000 men fights another equal in number, there are about 20,000 of them so diseased on each side."

"Very surprising indeed," said Candide, "but you must get cured." "Lord help me! how can I?" cried Pangloss. "My dear friend, I have not a penny in the world; and you know one cannot be bled or have an enema without a fee."

This last speech had its effect on Candide. He flew to the charitable Anabaptist James. He flung himself at his feet, and gave him so striking a picture of the miserable situation of his friend, that the good man, without any further hesitation, agreed to take Dr. Pangloss into his house and to pay for his cure. During the course of the cure Pangloss lost only one eye and one ear. Since his handwriting was good and he understood accounts tolerably well, the Anabaptist made him his bookkeeper. At the end of two months, being obliged to go to Lisbon about some mercantile affairs, he took the two philosophers with him in the same ship. Pangloss during the course of the voyage explained to him how everything was so constituted that it could not be better. James did not quite agree with him on this point. "Mankind," said he, "must in some things have deviated from their original innocence; for they were not born wolves, and yet they worry one another like those beasts of prey. God never gave them twenty-four pounders nor bayonets, and yet they have made cannon and bayonets to destroy one another. To this list I might add not only bankruptcies, but the law which seizes on the effects of bankrupts, only to cheat the creditors."[4] "All this was indispensably necessary," replied the one-eyed doctor; "for private misfortunes are public benefits; so that the more

---

*Mercenaries; professional soldiers hired to serve in foreign armies.

private misfortunes there are the greater is the general good." While
he was arguing in this manner the sky was overcast, the winds blew
from the four quarters of the compass, and the ship was assailed by
a most terrible tempest within sight of the port of Lisbon.

V

A Tempest, a Shipwreck, an Earthquake, and what else happened to Dr. Pangloss, Candide, and James the Anabaptist

One-half of the passengers, weakened and half-dead with the inconceivable anxiety and sickness which the rolling of a vessel at sea occasions through the whole human frame, were incapable of noticing the danger that surrounded them. The other half made loud outcries, or fell to their prayers. The sails were ripped to shreds, and the masts were toppled. The vessel was a perfect wreck. Everyone was busily employed, but nobody could be either heard or obeyed. The Anabaptist, being upon deck, lent a helping hand as well as the rest, when a brutish sailor struck him and knocked him to the deck; but from the violence of the blow the sailor himself tumbled headfirst overboard, and fell upon a piece of the broken mast, which he immediately grasped. Honest James, forgetting the injury he had just received from him, flew to his assistance, and with great difficulty hauled him in again, but in the attempt was, by a sudden jerk of the ship, thrown overboard himself, in sight of the very fellow whom he had risked his life to save, and who took not the least notice of him in this distress. Candide, who saw everything that had happened, and saw his benefactor one moment rising above water and the next swallowed up by the merciless waves, was preparing to jump in after him, but was prevented by the philosopher Pangloss, who demonstrated to him that the coast of Lisbon had been made on purpose for the Anabaptist to be drowned there. While he was proving his argument *à priori*,* the ship foundered, and the whole crew perished, except Pangloss, Candide, and the sailor who had caused the drowning of the good

---

*Argument based on theory rather than experience (Latin); Voltaire considered it characteristic of Leibnizian reasoning and philosophy.

Anabaptist. The villain swam ashore, but Pangloss and Candide got to land upon a plank.

As soon as they had recovered themselves from their surprise and fatigue, they walked towards Lisbon. With what little money they had left they hoped to save themselves from starving after having escaped drowning.

Scarcely had they finished lamenting the loss of their benefactor and set foot in the city, when they felt the earth tremble under their feet, and the sea, swelling and foaming in the harbour, dash in pieces the vessels that were anchored. Large sheets of flame and cinders covered the streets and public places. The houses tottered, and were tumbled, even to their foundations, which were themselves destroyed; and thirty thousand inhabitants of both sexes, young and old, were buried beneath the ruins.[5] The sailor, whistling and swearing, cried: "Damn it, there's something to be got here!" "What can be the 'sufficient reason' of this phenomenon?" said Pangloss. "It is certainly the Day of Judgment," said Candide. The sailor, defying death in the pursuit of plunder, rushed into the midst of the ruin, where he found some money, with which he got drunk, and after he had slept off the alcohol, he purchased the favours of the first good-natured wench that came his way, amidst the ruins of demolished houses and the groans of half-buried and expiring persons. Pangloss pulled him by the sleeve: "Friend," said he, "this is not right; you trespass against the *universal reason*, and your behavior is untimely." "Bloody Hell!" answered the other, "I am a sailor and born at Batavia, and have trampled four times upon the crucifix in as many voyages to Japan;[6] get out of here with your *universal reason*."

In the meantime, Candide, who had been wounded by some pieces of stone that fell from the houses, lay stretched in the street, almost covered with rubbish. "For God's sake," said he to Pangloss, "get me a little wine and oil; I am dying." "This earthquake is nothing new," replied Pangloss; "the city of Lima in America experienced the same last year:* the same cause, the same effect; there is certainly a train of sulphur all the way underground from Lima

---

*There had also recently been a great earthquake in Lima, Peru.

to Lisbon."* "Nothing more probable," said Candide; "but for the love of God a little oil and wine." "Probable!" replied the philosopher. "I maintain that the thing is demonstrable." Candide fainted, and Pangloss fetched him some water from a neighbouring spring.

The next day, in searching among the ruins, they found a little food, with which restored their exhausted strength. After this they assisted the inhabitants in helping the distressed and wounded. Some whom they had humanely assisted gave them as good a dinner as could be expected under such terrible circumstances. The meal, indeed, was mournful, and the company moistened their bread with their tears; but Pangloss endeavoured to comfort them by affirming that things could not be otherwise than they were: "for," said he, "all this is for the very best end, for if there is a volcano† at Lisbon, it could be in no other spot; for it is impossible but things should be as they are, for everything is for the best."

By the side of the preceptor sat a little man dressed in black, who was one of the familiars of the Inquisition.[7] This person, taking him up with great complaisance, said: "Possibly, my good sir, you do not believe in original sin; for if everything is best, there could have been no such thing as the fall or punishment of men."‡

"I humbly ask your excellency's pardon," answered Pangloss, still more politely; "for the fall of man, and the consequent curse, necessarily entered into the system of the best of worlds." "That is as much as to say, sir," rejoined the familiar, "you do not believe in free-will."[8] "Your excellency will be so good as to excuse me," said Pangloss; "free-will is consistent with absolute necessity; for it was necessary we should be free, for in that the will—"

Pangloss was in the midst of his proposition when the Inquisitor beckoned to his attendant to help him to a glass of port wine.

---

* Widespread theory regarding the cause of earthquakes.
† Reference to yet another current theory regarding earthquakes.
‡ Reference to the Bible, Genesis 3.

VI

How the Portuguese made a superb auto-da-fé[9] to prevent any future Earthquakes, and how Candide was publicly whipped

After the earthquake, which had destroyed three-fourths of the city of Lisbon, the sages of that country could think of no means more effectual to preserve the kingdom from utter ruin than to entertain the people with an *auto-da-fé*, it having been decided by the University of Coimbra that burning a few people alive by a slow fire, and with great ceremony, is an infallible secret for preventing earthquakes.

In consequence, they had rounded up a Biscayner for marrying his godmother,[10] and two Portuguese who while eating a chicken had set aside a piece of bacon used for seasoning;[11] after dinner, they came and secured Dr. Pangloss and his pupil Candide, the one for speaking his mind, and the other for seeming to approve what he said. They were taken separately to extremely cool apartments where they were never bothered by the glare of the sun.* Eight days afterwards they were each dressed in a *san-benito*,† and their heads were adorned with paper mitres.‡ The mitre and *san-benito* worn by Candide were painted with upside-down flames and with devils that had neither tails nor claws; but Dr. Pangloss's devils had both tails and claws, and his flames were upright.[12] In these costumes they marched in procession, and heard a very pathetic sermon, which was followed by an anthem accompanied by bagpipes. Candide was flogged to the cadence of the anthem; the Biscayner and the two men who would not eat bacon were burnt; and Pangloss was hanged, though hangings were not a common custom at these solem-

---

*Ironical description of prison cells.

†Yellow robe worn by heretics whom the Inquisition condemned to be burned at the stake.

‡Cone-shaped cap meant to resemble a bishop's ceremonial headdress.

28

nities. The same day there was another earthquake, which caused most dreadful havoc.*

Candide, amazed, terrified, confounded, astonished, all bloody and trembling from head to foot, said to himself: "If this is the best of all possible worlds, what are the others like? If I had only been whipped, I could have put up with it, as I did among the Bulgarians; but oh my dear Pangloss! my beloved master! thou greatest of philosophers! that ever I should live to see thee hanged, for no reason I can see! O my dear Anabaptist, thou best of men, that it should be your fate to be drowned in the harbour! O Miss Cunégonde, you mirror of young ladies! that it should be your fate to be ripped open!"

He was making the best of his way from the place where he had been preached to, whipped, absolved, and received benediction, when an old woman approached him and said: "Take courage, child, and follow me."

---

*There was indeed a second earthquake, on December 21, 1755.

VII

How the Old Woman took care of Candide, and how he found the Object of his Love

Candide followed the old woman, though without taking courage, to a decayed house, where she gave him a jar of ointment for his sores, showed him a very neat bed with a suit of clothes hanging up by it, and set some food and drink before him. "There," she said, "eat, drink, and sleep; and may our Blessed Lady of Atocha,* and the great St. Anthony of Padua,† and the illustrious St. James of Compostella‡ take you under their protection. I will be back to-morrow." Candide, struck with amazement at what he had seen, at what he had suffered, and still more with the charity of the old woman, would have shown his acknowledgment by kissing her hand. "It is not my hand you ought to kiss," said the old woman; "I will be back to-morrow. Rub your back with the ointment, eat, and take your rest."

Candide, in spite of his sufferings, ate and slept. The next morning the old woman brought him breakfast, examined his back, and rubbed it herself with another ointment. She returned at the proper time and brought him lunch, and at night she visited him again with supper. The next day she repeated the routine. "Who are you?" said Candide to her. "What God has inspired you with so much goodness? How can I repay you for this charitable assistance?" The good old woman kept a profound silence. In the evening she returned, but without his supper. "Come along with me," said she, "but do not speak a word." She took him under her arm, and walked with him about a quarter of a mile into the country, till

---

*Shrine in Madrid.

†Patron saint of Portugal and Padua.

‡According to tradition, he preached in Spain; his shrine at Santiago de Compostella became a renowned place of pilgrimage.

they came to a lonely house surrounded with moats and gardens. The old woman knocked at a little door, which was immediately opened, and she took him up a pair of back-stairs into a small but richly furnished apartment. There she made him sit down on a brocaded sofa; she closed the door, and left him. Candide thought he was in a trance; he looked upon his whole life up to this point as a frightful dream, and the present moment a very agreeable one.

The old woman soon returned, supporting, with great difficulty, a young lady, who appeared scarcely able to stand. She was of a majestic mein and stature, her dress was rich and glittering with diamonds, and her face was covered with a veil. "Take off that veil," said the old woman to Candide. The young man approached, and with a trembling hand took off her veil. What a happy moment! What surprise! He thought he beheld Miss Cunégonde. He did behold her: it was she herself! His strength failed him, he could not utter a word, he fell at her feet. Cunégonde fainted upon the sofa. The old woman revived them with alcohol; they recovered; they began to speak. At first they could express themselves only in broken accents; their questions and answers were alternately interrupted with sighs, tears, and exclamations. The old woman warned them to make less noise, and after this prudent admonition, left them together. "Good heavens!" cried Candide, "is it you? Is it Miss Cunégonde I see before me, alive? Do I find you again in Portugal? Then you have not been ravished? They did not rip you open as the philosopher Pangloss informed me?" "Indeed, but they did," replied Miss Cunégonde; "but these two accidents do not always prove mortal." "But were your father and mother killed?" "Alas!" answered she, "it is but too true!" and she wept. "And your brother?" "And my brother also." "And why are you in Portugal? And how did you know I was here? And by what strange adventure did you contrive to have me brought in to this house? And how—" "I will tell you all," replied the lady; "but first you must tell me about everything that has happened to you since the innocent kiss you gave me, and the rude kicking you received because of it."

Candide, with the greatest submission, prepared to obey the commands of his fair mistress, and though he was still wrapt in amazement, though his voice was low and tremulous, though his back pained him, yet he gave her a most ingenious account of every-

thing that had happened to him since the moment of their separa-
tion. Cunégonde, with her eyes lifted to heaven, shed tears when
he related the death of the good Anabaptist James, and of Pangloss;
after which she related her adventures to Candide, who lost not one
syllable she uttered, and seemed to devour her with his eyes all the
time she was speaking.[13]

VIII
The History of Cunégonde

I was in bed and fast asleep when heaven chose to send the Bulgarians to our delightful castle of Thunder-ten-tronckh, where they murdered my father and brother, and cut my mother in pieces. A tall Bulgarian soldier, six feet high, seeing that I had fainted at this sight, attempted to ravish me. At that I recovered my senses. I cried, I struggled, I bit, I scratched, I would have torn the tall Bulgarian's eyes out, not knowing that what had happened at my father's castle was a customary thing. The brutal soldier, enraged at my resistance, gave me a cut in the left groin with his knife, the mark of which I still carry." "I long to see it," said Candide, with all imaginable simplicity. "You shall," said Cunégonde; "but let me proceed." "Please do," replied Candide.

She continued: "A Bulgarian captain came in, and saw me covered in my blood, and the soldier still as busy as if no one had been present. The officer, enraged at the fellow's lack of respect to him, killed him with one stroke of his sabre. This captain took care of me, had me cured, and carried me as a prisoner of war to his quarters. I washed what little linen he owned and prepared his food. He was very fond of me, that was certain; neither can I deny that he was handsome, and had a white soft skin; but he was very stupid, and knew nothing of philosophy. It was evident that he had not been educated under Dr. Pangloss. After three months, having lost all his money, and being tired of me, he sold me to a Jew named Don Issachar, who traded in Holland and Portugal, and was passionately fond of women. This Jew showed me great kindness, in hopes to gain my favours; but this got him nowhere with me. A modest woman may be once violated, but her virtue is greatly strengthened as a result. In order to keep me hidden, he brought me to this country house you now see. I have hitherto believed that nothing could equal the beauty of the castle of Thunder-ten-tronckh, but I found I was mistaken.

"The Grand Inquisitor saw me one day at mass, ogled me all the time of service, and when it was over sent to let me know he wanted to speak with me about some private business. I was taken to his palace, where I told him all my story. He pointed out that it was beneath a person of my birth to belong to an Israelite. A suggestion was then made to Don Issachar, that he should turn me over to his lordship. Don Issachar, being the court banker and a man of credit, did not want to go along with it. His lordship threatened him with an *auto-da-fé*; in short, my Jew was frightened into a bargain, and it was agreed between them that the house and myself should belong to both of them; that the Jew should have Monday, Wednesday, and the Sabbath to himself, and the Inquisitor the other four days of the week. This agreement has existed almost six months, but not without several quarrels about whether the space from Saturday night to Sunday morning belonged to the old or the new law. For my part, I have so far withstood them both, and truly I believe that this is the very reason why they are both so fond of me.

"Finally, to avert further earthquakes, and to intimidate Don Issachar, my Lord Inquisitor chose to celebrate an *auto-da-fé*. He did me the honour of inviting me to the ceremony. I had a very good seat; and refreshments of all kinds were offered the ladies between mass and the execution. I was dreadfully shocked at the burning of the two Jews and the honest Biscayner who married his godmother; but how great was my surprise, my consternation and concern, when I beheld a figure so like Pangloss, dressed in a *san-benito* and mitre! I rubbed my eyes, I looked at him attentively. I saw him hanged and I fainted. Scarcely had I recovered my senses when I saw you, stark naked: this was the peak of horror, grief and despair. I must confess to you for a truth, that your skin is far whiter and more delicate than that of the Bulgarian captain. This spectacle worked me up to a pitch of distraction. I screamed out, and would have said, 'Hold, barbarians!' but my voice failed me; and indeed my cries would have been useless. After you had been severely whipped, 'How is it possible,' I said to myself, 'that the lovely Candide and the sage Pangloss should be in Lisbon, the one to receive a hundred lashes, and the other to be hanged, by order of my Lord Inquisitor, whose mistress I am?' Pangloss deceived me most cruelly in saying that everything is fittest and best.

"Thus agitated and perplexed, now distracted and lost, now half-dead with grief, I revolved in my mind the murder of my father, mother, and brother, committed before my eyes; the insolence of the villainous Bulgarian soldier; the wound he gave me in the groin; my servitude; my being a cook wench to my Bulgarian captain; my subjection to the dirty Jew and my cruel Inquisitor; the hanging of Doctor Pangloss; the Miserere* sung while you were being whipped; and particularly the kiss I gave you behind the screen the last day I ever saw you. I returned thanks to God for having brought you back to me after so many trials. I charged the old woman who attends me to bring you here as soon as was convenient. She has punctually followed my orders, and I now enjoy the inexpressible satisfaction of seeing you, hearing you, and speaking to you. But you must certainly be half dead with hunger; I myself am very hungry; and so let us sit down to supper."

Upon this the two lovers immediately placed themselves at table, and after having eaten, they returned to the magnificent sofa already mentioned, where they were when Signor Don Issachar, one of the masters of the house, entered unexpectedly. It was the Sabbath-day, and he came to enjoy his privilege, and sigh forth his passion at the feet of the fair Cunégonde.

---

*Psalm 51 of the Bible; hymn of penitence invoking God's mercy.

IX

What happened to Cunégonde, Candide, the Grand Inquisitor, and the Jew

This same Issachar was the most choleric little Hebrew that had ever been in Israel since the captivity of Babylon.* "What's this," said he, "you Galilean wretch? The Inquisitor was not enough for you, but this rascal must come in for a share with me!" In uttering these words he drew out a long sword which he always carried about with him, and, supposing his adversary defenseless, he attacked him furiously; but our honest Westphalian had received a handsome sword from the old woman with his suit of clothes. Candide drew his sword, and though he was the most gentle, sweet-tempered young man breathing, he whipped it into the Israelite, and laid him sprawling on the floor at the fair Cunégonde's feet.

"Holy Virgin!" cried she, "what will become of us? A man killed in my apartment! If the police come we are done for." "Had not Pangloss been hanged," replied Candide, "he would have given us most excellent advice in this emergency, for he was a profound philosopher. But since he is not here let us consult the old woman." She was very understanding, and was beginning to give her advice, when another door opened suddenly. It was now one o'clock in the morning, and of course the beginning of Sunday, which, by agreement, belonged to my Lord Inquisitor. Entering, he discovered the whipped Candide, with his drawn sword in his hand, a dead body stretched on the floor, Cunégonde frightened out of her wits, and the old woman giving advice.

At that very moment thought came into Candide's head. "If this holy man," thought he, "should call for assistance, I shall most

---

*Jerusalem was captured by Nebuchadnezzar, king of Babylon, in 597 B.C.

THE RETURN OF DON ISSACHAR.

undoubtedly be condemned to be burned, and Miss Cunégonde may perhaps meet with no better treatment. Besides he was the cause of my being so cruelly whipped; he is my rival; and as I have now begun to dip my hands in blood, I will kill away, for there is no time to hesitate." This whole train of reasoning was clear and instantaneous; so that, without giving time to the Inquisitor to recover from his surprise, Candide stabbed him, and laid him by the side of the Jew. "Here's another fine piece of work!" cried Cunégonde. "Now there can be no hope for us; we'll be excommunicated; our last hour has come! But how could you, who are of so mild a temper, kill a Jew and Inquisitor in two minutes' time?" "Beautiful miss," answered Candide, "when a man is in love, is jealous, and has been whipped by the Inquisition, he is no longer himself."

The old woman then put in her word. "There were three Andalusian horses in the stable," said she, "with their bridles and saddles. Let the brave Candide get them ready; madame has a parcel of gold coins and jewels. Let's mount the horses immediately, though I have only one buttock to sit on. Let us set out for Cadiz; it is the finest weather in the world, and there is great pleasure in travelling in the cool of the night."

Candide, without any further hesitation, saddles the three horses; and Miss Cunégonde, the old woman and he set out, and travel thirty miles without a stop. While they were making the best of their way, the Holy Brotherhood* entered the house. My Lord the Inquisitor was buried in a magnificent manner; and Master Issachar's body was thrown upon a dunghill.

Candide, Cunégonde, and the old woman had by this time reached the little town of Avecina, in the midst of the mountains of Sierra Morena, and were engaged in the following conversation in an inn where they were staying.

*Powerful religious order in Spain with a police force for pursuing criminals.

X

In what distress Candide, Cunégonde, and the Old Woman arrived at Cadiz; and of their Embarkation

"Who could it be that has robbed me of my gold coins and jewels?" exclaimed Miss Cunégonde, all bathed in tears. "How will we live? what will we do? where will I find Inquisitors and Jews who can give me more?" "Alas!" said the old woman, "I have a shrewd suspicion of a reverend Father Cordelier, who shared the same inn with us last night at Badajoz. God forbid I should condemn any one wrongfully, but he came into our room twice, and he set off in the morning long before us."

"Alas!" said Candide, "Pangloss has often proved to me that the goods of this world are common to all men, and that every one has an equal right to the enjoyment of them;* but according to these principles, the Cordelier should have left us enough to carry us to the end of our journey. Have you nothing at all left, my dear Miss Cunégonde?" "Not a sous,"† replied she. "What can we do, then?" said Candide. "Sell one of the horses," replied the old woman. "I will ride behind Miss Cunégonde, though I have only one buttock to ride on; and we shall reach Cadiz, never fear."

In the same inn there was a Benedictine friar, who bought the horse very cheap. Candide, Cunégonde, and the old woman, after passing through Lucina, Chellas, and Letrixa, arrived finally at Cadiz. A fleet was then getting ready, and troops were assembling, in order to reason with the Jesuit fathers of Paraguay, who were accused of

---

*Possible allusion to Jean-Jacques Rousseau's *Discourse on the Origin and the Foundations of Inequality Among Mankind* (1754); Voltaire disagreed with its egalitarian thesis.
†Meaning "not a cent."

having excited one of the Indian tribes in the neighbourhood of the town of the Holy Sacrament to revolt against the kings of Spain and Portugal.[14] Candide, having been in the Bulgarian army, performed the Bulgarian military exercises before the general of this little army with so intrepid an air, and with such agility and expedition, that he gave him an infantry company to command. Being now made a captain, he sailed with Miss Cunégonde, the old woman, two valets, and the two Andalusian horses which had belonged to the Grand Inquisitor of Portugal.

During their voyage they amused themselves with many profound reasonings on poor Pangloss's philosophy. "We are now going into another world, and surely it must be there that everything is best; for I must confess that we have had some reason to complain of what passes in ours, in regard to both our physical and moral states. Though I have a sincere love for you," said Miss Cunégonde, "I still shudder at the thought of what I have seen and experienced." "All will be well," replied Candide. "The sea of this new world is already better than our European seas; it is smoother, and the winds blow more regularly." "God grant it," said Cunégonde. "But I have met with such terrible treatment in this that I have almost lost all hopes of a better." "What murmurings and complainings indeed!" cried the old woman. "If you had suffered half what I have done there might be some reason for it." Miss Cunégonde could scarcely refrain laughing at the good old woman, and thought it droll enough to pretend to a greater share of misfortune than herself. "Alas! you poor old thing," said she, "unless you have been ravished by two Bulgarians, had received two deep wounds in your body, had seen two of your own castles demolished, had lost two fathers and two mothers, and seen both of them barbarously murdered before your eyes, and to sum up all, had two lovers whipped at an *auto-da-fé*, I cannot see how you could be more unfortunate than I. Add to this, though born a baroness, and bearing seventy-two quarterings, I have been reduced to a cook-wench." "Miss," replied the old woman, "you do not know my birth and rank; but if I were to show you everything, you would not talk in this manner, but would suspend your judgment." This speech inspired a great curiosity in Candide and Cunégonde, and the old woman continued as follows.

XI

The History of the Old Woman

I have not always been bleary-eyed; my nose did not always touch my chin; nor was I always a servant. You must know that I am the daughter of Pope Urban X and of the Princess of Palestrina.[15] Until the age of fourteen I was brought up in a castle so splendid that all the castles of your German barons would not have served it as a stable, and one of my robes would have bought half the province of Westphalia. I grew up, and improved in beauty, wit, and every graceful accomplishment; and in the midst of pleasures, dignities and the highest expectations. I was already inspiring young men to love. My breast began to take its right form: and such a breast—white, firm, and formed like that of Venus of Medicis. My eyebrows were as black as jet; and as for my eyes, they darted flames, and eclipsed the lustre of the stars, as I was told by the poets of our part of the world. My maids, when they dressed and undressed me, used to fall into an ecstasy whether viewing me from in front or behind; and all the men longed to be in their places.

I was engaged to a sovereign prince of Massa Carara. Such a prince! as handsome as myself, sweet-tempered, agreeable, witty, and in love with me madly. I loved him too, as one loves for the first time, with devotion approaching idolatry. The wedding preparations were made with surprising splendour and magnificence; there were feasts, carousals, and burlettas; all Italy composed sonnets in my praise, though not one of them was tolerable. I was on the point of reaching the summit of bliss, when an old marquise, who had been mistress to the prince my husband, invited him to drink a cup of chocolate. In less than two hours after he returned from the visit, he died of the most terrible convulsions. But this is a mere trifle. My mother, distracted to the highest degree, and yet less afflicted than I, determined to escape for some time from the funereal

THE TOILET OF THE POPE'S DAUGHTER

atmosphere. As she had a very fine estate in the neighbourhood of Gaieta,* we embarked on board a galley, which was gilded like the high altar of St Peter's at Rome. At sea, we were raided by a pirate ship from Salé.† Our men defended themselves like true pope's soldiers; they flung themselves upon their knees, laid down their weapons, and begged the corsair to give them absolution in *articulo mortis*.‡

The Moors presently stripped us as naked as monkeys. My mother, my maids of honour, and myself were all treated in the same manner. It is amazing how quick these gentry are at undressing people. But what surprised me most was, that they thrust their fingers into every part of our bodies that their fingers could in any way reach. I thought it a very strange kind of ceremony; for that is how we are generally apt to judge of things when we have not seen the world. I learnt afterwards that it was to discover if we had no diamonds concealed. This practice has been long-standing among those civilised nations that scour the seas. I was informed that the religious Knights of Malta never fail to make this search whenever any Moors of either sex fall into their hands. It is one of those international laws from which they never deviate.

I need not tell you how great a hardship it was for a young princess and her mother to be made slaves and carried to Morocco. You may easily imagine that we must have suffered on board the pirate ship. My mother was still extremely handsome, our maids of honour, and even our common waiting-women had more charms than were to be found in all Africa. As to myself, I was enchanting; I was beauty itself, and then I had my innocence. But alas! I did not retain it long; this precious flower, which was reserved for the lovely prince of Massa Carara, was plucked by the captain of the Moorish vessel, who was a hideous negro, and thought he did me infinite honour. Indeed, both the Princess of Palestrina and myself must have been very strong indeed to undergo all the hardships and violences we suffered till our arrival at Morocco. But I will not detain

---

*Approximately halfway between Rome and Naples.
†A rover is a pirate ship; Salé, on the coast of Morocco, was a center of piracy in the eighteenth century.
‡At the point of death (Latin).

you any longer with such common things; they are hardly worth mentioning.

Upon our arrival at Morocco we found that kingdom bathed in blood. Fifty sons of the Emperor Muley Ishmael* were each at the head of a party. This produced fifty civil wars of blacks against blacks, of browns against browns, and of mulattoes against mulattoes. In short, the whole empire was one continued scene of carcases.

No sooner were we landed than a party of blacks, of a faction hostile to my captain, came to rob him of his booty. After the money and jewels we were the most valuable things he had. I was witness on this occasion to such a battle as you never see in your cold European climates. The northern nations do not have the hot blood, nor that raging lust for women that is so common in Africa. The natives of Europe seem to have their veins filled with milk only; but fire and vitrol circulate in those of the inhabitants of Mount Atlas and the neighbouring provinces. They fought with the fury of the lions, tigers and serpents of their country, to decide who should have us. A Moor seized my mother by the right arm, while my captain's lieutenant held her by the left; another Moor laid hold of her by the right leg, and one of our corsairs held her by the other. In this manner were almost every one of our women dragged between four soldiers. My captain kept me concealed behind him, and with his scymetar cut down every one who opposed him; at length I saw all our Italian women and my mother mangled and torn to pieces by the monsters who were fighting over them. The captives, my companions, the Moors who took us, the soldiers, the sailors, the blacks, the whites, the mulattoes, and lastly, my captain himself, were all slain, and I remained alone, half-dead upon a heap of dead bodies. Similar barbarous scenes were occurring every day over the whole country, which is an extent of three hundred leagues, and yet they never missed the five stated times of prayer decreed by their prophet Mahomet.

I untangled myself with great difficulty from this vast heap of

---

*Sultan of Morocco who lived from 1646 to 1727 and reigned for fifty years; civil war and bloody strife followed his death.

slaughtered bodies, and crawled to a large orange tree that stood on the bank of a neighbouring rivulet, where I fell down exhausted with fatigue, and overwhelmed with horror, despair and hunger. My senses being overpowered, I fell asleep, or rather seemed to be in a trance. Thus I lay in a state of weakness and insensibility, between life and death, when I felt myself touched by something that moved up and down upon my body. This brought me to myself; I opened my eyes, and saw an attractive, fair-faced man, who sighed, and muttered these words between his teeth: "O che sciagura d'essere senza coglioni!"*

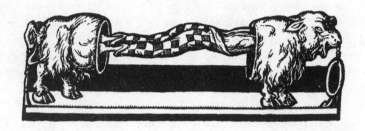

---

* "Oh, what a misfortune to be without balls!" (Italian). The man who utters these words is a castrato, a singer emasculated as a boy to preserve the soprano or contralto range of his voice.

XII

The Adventures of the Old Woman (continued)

Astonished and delighted to hear my native language, and no
less surprised at the young man's words, I told him that there
were far greater misfortunes in the world than what he complained of. And to convince him of it, I gave him a short history
of the horrible disasters that had happened to me; and, as soon as
I had finished, I fainted again. He carried me in his arms to a neighbouring cottage, where he had me put to bed, gave me something
to eat, waited on me with the greatest attention, comforted me,
caressed me, told me that he had never seen anything so perfectly
beautiful as myself, and that he had never so much regretted the
loss of what no one could restore to him. "I was born at Naples,"
he said, "where they castrate two or three thousand children every
year; several die of the operation; some acquire voices far beyond
the most tuneful of your ladies; and others are sent to govern states
and empires.* My operation was a great success, and I was one of
the singers in the Princess of Palestrina's chapel." "In my mother's
chapel!" I exclaimed. "The Princess of Palestrina, your mother!"
cried he, bursting into a flood of tears. "You must be the beautiful
young princess whom I raised till she was six years old, and who
at that tender age promised to be as fair as you are now?" "I am
the same," I replied: "my mother lies about a hundred yards from
here, cut in pieces, and buried under a heap of dead bodies."

I then related to him all that had happened to me, and he, in
return, acquainted me with all his adventures, and how he had been
sent to the court of the King of Morocco by a Christian prince,[16] to
conclude a treaty with that monarch; the result of which granted

---

*Allusion to the famous Italian *castrato* Carlo Broschi, known as Farinelli (1705–
1782).

him gunpowder, cannon, and ships to enable him to destroy the commerce of other Christian governments. "My mission is concluded," said the eunuch; "I am going to take ship at Ceuta, and I'll take you along with me to Italy. 'Ma che sciagura d'essere senza coglioni!' "

I thanked him with tears of joy; and instead of taking me with him into Italy, he carried me into Algiers, and sold me to the Dey of that province. I had not been long a slave, when the plague, which had made the tour of Africa, Asia, and Europe, broke out at Algiers with redoubled fury. You have seen an earthquake; but tell me, miss, have you ever the plague? "Never," answered the young baroness.

If you ever had (continued the old woman) you would admit that an earthquake was a trifle compared to it. It is very common in Africa; I was seized with it. Imagine, if you will, the distressed situation of the daughter of a pope, only fifteen years old, and who in less than three months had felt the miseries of poverty and slavery; had been ravished almost every day; had beheld her mother cut into four quarters; had experienced the scourges of famine and war, and was now dying of the plague at Algiers. I did not, however, die of it; but my eunuch and the Dey,* and almost the whole seraglio of Algiers, perished.

As soon as the first fury of this dreadful pestilence was over, a sale was made of the Dey's slaves. I was purchased by a merchant, who carried me to Tunis. This man sold me to another merchant, who sold me again to another at Tripoli; from Tripoli I was sold to Alexandria, from Alexandria to Smyrna, and from Smyrna to Constantinople. After many changes, I ended up the property of an aga of the janissaries,† who, soon after I came into his possession, was ordered away to the defence of Asoph, then besieged by the Russians.‡

The aga, being very fond of women, took his whole seraglio

---

*Former title of the governor of Algiers.

†An aga is an important Turkish official; the janisseries were an elite corps of Turkish troops.

‡Reference to Asov, near the mouth of the Don; besieged by Peter the Great in 1695 and 1696.

with him, and lodged us in a small fort, with two black eunuchs and twenty soldiers to guard us. Our army killed a huge number of Russians; but they soon returned us the compliment. Asoph was taken by storm, and the enemy spared neither age nor sex, but put all to the sword, and laid the city in ashes. Our little fort alone held out; they resolved to reduce us by famine. The twenty janissaries who were left to defend it, had sworn never to surrender the place. Being reduced to the extremity of famine, they found themselves obliged to kill our two eunuchs, and eat them, rather than violate their oath. After a few more days, they resolved to eat the women too.

We had a very pious and humane imam,* who delivered an excellent sermon on this occasion, persuading them not to kill us at once; "Only cut off one of the buttocks of each of those ladies," said he, "and you will fare extremely well; if you still need more you can come back in a few days and have the same. Heaven will approve of so charitable an action, and you will be saved."

By the force of this eloquence he easily persuaded them, and all underwent the operation. The imam applied the same balsam as they do to children after circumcision. We were all at the point of death.

The janissaries had scarcely time to finish the repast with which we had supplied them, when the Russians appeared in flat-bottomed boats; not a single janissary escaped. The Russians paid no regard to the condition we were in; but as there are French surgeons in all parts of the world, a skillful operator took us under his care, and cured us; and I will never forget for as long as I live, that as soon as my wounds were perfectly healed he made me certain proposals. In general, he desired us all to have a good heart, assuring us that the same thing had happened in many sieges and that it was agreeable to the laws of war.

As soon as my companions were in a condition to walk, they were sent to Moscow. As for me, I fell to the lot of a boyard,† who put me to work in his garden, and gave me twenty lashes a day.

---

*Muslim religious leader (Arabic).
†Member of the aristocracy in czarist Russia.

But when this nobleman was broken on the wheel after about two years, with about thirty others, for some court intrigues,* I took advantage of the event and made my escape. I travelled over a great part of Russia. I was for a long time an innkeeper's servant at Riga, then at Rostock, Wismar, Leipsick, Cassel, Utrecht, Leyden, the Hague, and Rotterdam: I have grown old in misery and disgrace, living with only one buttock, and in remembering always that I was a pope's daughter. I have been a hundred times on the point of killing myself, but still was fond of life. This ridiculous weakness is perhaps one of our worst instincts. What can be more absurd than choosing to carry a burden that one really wants to throw to the ground? To detest, and yet to strive to preserve our existence? To caress the serpent that devours us, and hug him close to our bosoms till he has gnawed into our hearts?

In the different countries in which it has been my fate to wander, and the many inns where I have been a servant, I have observed a prodigious number of people who held their existence in abhorrence, and yet I never knew more than twelve who voluntarily put an end to their misery: namely, three negroes, four Englishmen, four Genoese, and a German professor named Robek.[17] My last place was with the Jew, Don Issachar, who attached me to your service, my fair lady; to whose destinies I have attached myself, and have been more concerned with your misfortunes than with my own. I would never have even mentioned the matter to you, if you had not irked me a little bit; and if it was not customary to tell stories on board a ship in order to pass away the time. In short, my dear miss, I have a great deal of knowledge and experience in the world; therefore, take my advice—divert yourself, and ask each passenger to tell his story, and if there is one of them all who has not cursed his existence many times, and said to himself over and over again that he was the most miserable of men, I give you permission to throw me head-first into the sea.

---

*Reference to an unsuccessful conspiracy against Peter the Great and his terrible reprisals, which took place in 1698.

XIII

How Candide was obliged to leave the fair Cunégonde and the Old Woman

The fair Cunégonde, having heard the history of the old woman's life and adventures, paid her all the respect and civility due to a person of her rank and merit. She very readily accepted her proposal of engaging every one of the passengers to relate their adventures in their turns, and was at length, as well as Candide, compelled to acknowledge that the old woman was right. "It is a thousand pities," said Candide, "that the sage Pangloss should have been hanged contrary to the custom of an *auto-da-fé*, for he would have read us a most admirable lecture on the moral and physical evil which cover the earth and sea; and I think I might have courage enough to presume to offer, with all due respect, some few objections."

While every one was reciting his adventures, the ship continued on her way, and at length arrived at Buenos Ayres, where Cunégonde, Captain Candide, and the old woman landed, and went to wait upon the Governor, Don Fernando d'Ibaraa y Figueora y Mascarenes y Lampourdos y Souza. This nobleman carried himself with a haughtiness suitable to a person who bore so many names. He spoke with the most noble disdain to every one, carried his nose so high, strained his voice to such a pitch, assumed so imperious an air, and stalked with so much loftiness and pride, that every one who had the honour of conversing with him was violently tempted to kick his excellency. He was immoderately fond of women, and Miss Cunégonde appeared in his eyes a paragon of beauty. The first thing he did was to ask her if she was the captain's wife. The air with which he made this demand alarmed Candide, who did not dare to say he was married to her, because indeed he was not; neither did he dare say she was his sister, because she was not; and though a lie of this nature proved of great service to one of the

ancients,* and might possibly be useful to some of the moderns,
yet the purity of his heart would not permit him to violate the truth.
"Miss Cunégonde," replied he, "is to do me the honour of marrying
me, and we humbly beseech your excellency to perform the ceremony for us."

Don Fernando d'Ibaraa y Figueora y Mascarenes y Lampourdos y
Souza, twirling his mustachio, and putting on a sarcastic smile, ordered Captain Candide to go and drill his company. The gentle
Candide obeyed, and the Governor was left with Miss Cunégonde.
He made her a strong declaration of love, protesting that he would
marry her tomorrow in the face of the Church, or otherwise, as
should appear most agreeable to a young lady of her prodigious
beauty. Cunégonde asked to retire for a quarter of an hour to consult
the old woman, and determine how she should proceed.

The old woman gave her the following counsel: "Miss, you have
seventy-two quarterings in your arms, it is true, but you do not
have a penny. It is your own fault if you are not wife to one of the
greatest nobleman in South America, with an exceedingly fine mustachio. Are you going to insist on an absolute fidelity? You have
been ravished by a Bulgarian soldier; a Jew and an Inquisitor have
both tasted of your favours. People take advantage of misfortunes.
I must confess, if I were in your place I would without the least
scruple give my hand to the Governor, and make the fortune of the
brave Captain Candide." While the old woman was thus haranguing,
with all the prudence that old age and experience furnish, a small
ship entered the harbour, bearing an alcayde† and his alguazils.‡ And
here is what happened:

The old woman rightly guessed that the Cordelier with the long
sleeves was the person who had taken Miss Cunégonde's money and
jewels, while they and Candide were at Badajoz in their flight from
Lisbon. This same friar attempted to sell some of the diamonds to
a jeweller, who recognized them as belonging to the Grand Inquisitor, and stopped them. The Cordelier, before he was hanged, ac-

---

*Ironical reference to the Bible, Genesis 12:12–13, where Abraham lies to the Egyp-
tians, telling them that Sarah was his sister and not his wife.
†Municipal judge or officer (Spanish).
‡Police officers (Spanish).

knowledged that he had stolen them, and described the persons and the road they had taken. The flight of Cunégonde and Candide was already known. They were traced to Cadiz; and the vessel which had been hastily dispatched in pursuit of them now reached the port of Buenos Ayres. A rumor spread that an alcayde was going to land, and that he was in pursuit of the murderers of my lord the Inquisitor. The sage old woman immediately saw what was to be done. "You cannot run away," said she to Cunégonde; "you have nothing to fear. It was not you who killed my Lord Inquisitor. Besides, as the Governor is in love with you, he will not allow you to be ill-treated. Therefore, stand your ground." Then hurrying away to Candide, "Flee," said she, "this instant, or you will be burnt alive!" Candide found there was no time to be lost. But how could he part from Cunégonde, and where must he go for shelter?

XIV

How Candide and Cacambo were received by the Jesuits in Paraguay

Candide had brought with him from Cadiz such a footman as one often meets with on the coast of Spain and in the Colonies. He was one-quarter Spanish, the son of a half-breed and was born in Tucuman.* He had been a singing boy, sexton, sailor, monk, pedlar, soldier, and lackey. His name was Cacambo. He had a great affection for his master, because his master was a very good man. He immediately saddled the two Andalusian horses. "Come, my good master, let's follow the old woman's advice, and hurry to leave this place without a backward glance." Candide burst into a flood of tears: "Oh, my dear Cunégonde, must I leave you just as the governor was going to marry us? Cunégonde, so long lost and found again, what will now become of you?" "Lord," said Cacambo, "she must do as well as she can: women are never at a loss. God takes care of them, and so let's get going." "But where will you take me? Where can we go? What can we do without Cunégonde?" cried the disconsolate Candide. "By St James of Compostella," said Cacambo "you were going to fight against the Jesuits of Paraguay; now let's go and fight for them. I know the road perfectly well; I'll take you to their kingdom; they will be delighted with a captain that understands the Bulgarian drill; you will certainly make a prodigious fortune. If we cannot find our account in one world, we'll find it in another. It is a great pleasure to see new objects and perform new exploits."

"Then you have been to Paraguay," said Candide. "Indeed I have," replied Cacambo. "I was a cook in the College of the As-

---

*In other words, he was part South American Indian and part European; Tucuman is a province in northern Argentina.

sumption, and I know the new government of Los Padres* as well
as I know the streets of Cadiz. Oh, it is an admirable government,
that is most certain! The kingdom is at present more than three
hundred leagues in diameter, and divided into thirty provinces; Los
Padres own everything there, and the people have no money at all.
This you must allow is the masterpiece of justice and reason. For
my part, I see nothing so divine as Los Padres, who wage war in
this part of the world against the troops of Spain and Portugal, and
at the same time they hear the confessions of those very princes in
Europe who kill Spaniards in America, and in Madrid they send
them to heaven. This pleases me exceedingly; but let us get going;
you are going to see the happiest and most fortunate of all mortals.
How charmed will Los Padres be to hear that a captain who understands the Bulgarian drill is coming."

As soon as they reached the first barrier, Cacambo called to the
advance-guard, and told them that a captain wanted to speak to my
lord the general. Notice was given to the main-guard, and immediately a Paraguayan officer ran to throw himself at the feet of the
commandant, to impart this news to him. Candide and Cacambo
were immediately disarmed, and their two Andalusian horses were
seized. The two strangers were placed between two files of soldiers.
The commandant was at the farther end with a three-cornered cap
on his head, his gown tucked up, a sword by his side, and a half-
pike in his hand. He made a sign, and instantly twenty-four soldiers
surrounded the new-comers. A sergeant told them that they must
wait, the commander could not speak to them; and that the reverend
father provincial had forbidden any Spaniard to open his mouth
except in his presence, or to stay longer than three hours in the
province. "And where is the reverend father provincial?" said Cacambo. "He has just said mass, and is at the parade," replied the
sergeant, "and in about three hours time you may possibly have the
honour of kissing his spurs." "But," said Cacambo, "the captain,
who as well as myself is dying of hunger, is no Spaniard but a
German; can't we have some breakfast while waiting for his rev-
erence?"

---

* The Jesuit fathers.

The sergeant immediately went off to report this speech to the commandant. "God be praised," said the reverend commandant; "since he is a German I will hear what he has to say; bring him to my arbour." They immediately led Candide to a beautiful pavilion adorned with a colonnade of green marble spotted with yellow, and with an inter-texture of vines, which served as a kind of cage for parrots, humming-birds, fly-birds, Guinea hens, and all other curious kinds of birds. An excellent breakfast was provided in vessels of gold, and while the Paraguayans were eating coarse Indian corn out of wooden dishes in the open air, and exposed to the burning heat of the sun, the reverend father commandant retired to his cool arbour.

He was a very handsome young man, round-faced, fair, and fresh-coloured, his eyebrows were finely arched, he had a piercing eye, the tips of his ears were red, his lips vermilion, and he had a bold and commanding air; but such a boldness as neither resembled that of a Spaniard nor of a Jesuit. Their confiscated weapons were returned to Candide and Cacambo, together with their two Andalusian horses. Cacambo gave the poor beasts some oats to eat close by the arbour, keeping a strict eye on them all the while for fear of ambush.

Candide first kissed the hem of the commandant's robe, then they sat down at the table. "It seems you are a German," says the Jesuit to him in that language. "Yes, reverend father," answered Candide. As they pronounced these words they looked at each other with great amazement, and with an emotion that neither could conceal. "Which part of Germany are you from?" said the Jesuit. "From the dirty province of Westphalia," answered Candide. "I was born in the castle of Thunder-ten-tronckh." "Oh heavens! is it possible?" said the commandant. "What a miracle!" cried Candide. "Can it be you?" said the commandant. At this they both fell back a few steps, then running into each other's arms, embraced, and let fall a shower of tears. "Is it you, then, reverend father? You are the brother of the fair Miss Cunégonde? you that were slain by the Bulgarians! you the baron's son! you a Jesuit in Paraguay! I must confess this is a strange world we live in. O Pangloss! Pangloss! what joy would this have given you if you had not been hanged."

The commandant dismissed the negro slaves and the Paraguayans, who presented them with liquor in crystal goblets. He returned thanks to God and St Ignatius a thousand times; he clasped Candide in his arms, and both their faces were bathed in tears. "You will be more surprised, more affected, more beside yourself," said Candide "when I tell you that Miss Cunégonde, your sister, whose body was supposed to have been ripped open, is in perfect health." "Where?" "In your neighborhood, with the governor of Buenos Ayres; and I myself was going to fight against you." Every word they uttered during this long conversation added some new matter of astonishment. Their souls fluttered on their tongues, listened in their ears and sparkled in their eyes. Like true Germans, they continued a long while at table, waiting for the reverend father, and the commandant spoke to his dear Candide as follows:

THE RESCUE OF THE BARON

XV

How Candide killed the Brother of his dear
Cunégonde

"Never while I live shall I lose the remembrance of that horrible day on which I saw my father and brother barbarously butchered before my eyes, and my sister ravished. When the Bulgarians retired we searched in vain for my dear sister. She was nowhere to be found; but the bodies of my father, mother and myself, with two maid-servants and three little boys, all of whom had been murdered by the remorseless enemy, were thrown into a cart to be buried in a chapel belonging to the Jesuits, within two leagues of our ancestral castle. A Jesuit sprinkled us with some holy water, which was horribly salty, and a few drops of it went into my eyes. The father perceived that my eyelids stirred a little; he put his hand upon my breast, and felt my heart beat; I was rescued and at the end of three weeks I had perfectly recovered. You know, my dear Candide, I was very handsome. I became still more so, and the reverend father Croust,* superior of that house, took a great fancy to me. He gave me the habit of the order, and some years afterwards I was sent to Rome. Our general needed new recruitments of young German Jesuits. The sovereigns of Paraguay admit of as few Spanish Jesuits as possible; they prefer those of other nations, whom they believe to be more obedient to command. The reverend father-general judged me fit to work in that vineyard. I set out with a Pole and a Tyrolese. Upon my arrival I was honoured with a sub-deaconship and a lieutenancy. Now I am colonel and priest. We shall give a warm reception to the King of Spain's troops;

---

*Father Antoine Kroust, rector at Colmar from 1753 to 1763, was hostile to Voltaire and the *philosophes*; Voltaire quarreled with him during his stay in that city in 1754.

I can assure you they will be well excommunicated and beaten. Providence has sent you hither to assist us. But is it true that my dear sister Cunégonde is in the neighbourhood with the governor of Buenos Ayres?" Candide swore that nothing could be more true; and the tears began to trickle down their cheeks again.

The baron knew no end of embracing Candide; he called him his brother, his deliverer. "Perhaps," said he, "my dear Candide, we shall be fortunate enough to enter the town sword in hand, and recover my sister Cunégonde." "Ah! that is all I desire," replied Candide, "for I intended to marry her; and I hope I shall still be able to." "Insolent fellow!" replied the baron. "You! you have the impudence to marry my sister, who bears seventy-two quarterings! Really I think you are very presumptuous to dare so much as to mention such an audacious design to me." Candide, thunderstruck at the oddness of this speech, answered: "Reverend father, all the quarterings in the world are of no significance. I have rescued your sister from a Jew and an Inquisitor; she is under many obligations to me, and she wants to marry me. My master Pangloss always told me that all people are by nature equal. Therefore, I will certainly marry your sister." "We will see about that, villain!" said the Jesuit baron of Thunder-ten-tronckh, and struck him across the face with the flat side of his sword. Candide in an instant drew his rapier, and plunged it up to the hilt in the Jesuit's body; but in pulling it out, reeking hot, he burst into tears. "Good God," cried he, "I have killed my old master, my friend, my brother-in-law. I am the best man in the world, and yet I have already killed three men; and of these three two were priests."

Cacambo, who was standing sentry near the door of the arbour, instantly ran up. "We can do nothing," said his master, "but sell our lives as dearly as possible. They will undoubtedly look into the arbour; we must die sword in hand." Cacambo, who had seen many of these kind of adventures, was not discouraged. He stripped the baron of his Jesuit's habit and put it upon Candide, then gave him the dead man's three-cornered cap, and made him mount on horseback. All this was done in the wink of an eye. "Gallop, master," cried Cacambo; "everybody will take you for a Jesuit going to give orders, and we will have passed the frontiers before they can overtake us." He flew as he spoke these words, crying out aloud in Spanish: "Make way! make way for the reverend father-colonel!"

XVI

What happened to our two Travellers
with two Girls, two Monkeys, and
the savages called Oreillons*

Candide and his valet had already passed the frontiers before
it was known that the German Jesuit was dead. The wary
Cacambo had taken care to fill his satchel with bread, chocolate, some ham, some fruit, and a few bottles of wine. They pushed
their Andalusian horses forward into a strange country, where there
were no roads. At length, a beautiful meadow, divided by several
streams, opened to their view. Cacambo suggested to his master that
they eat, and he promptly set the example. "How can you expect
me to feast upon ham when I have killed the baron's son, and am
doomed never more to see the beautiful Cunégonde? How will it
serve me to prolong a wretched life that might be spent far from
her in remorse and despair? And then what will the journal of Tre-
voux† say about all this?"

While he was making these reflections he still continued eating.
The sun was now at the point of setting when our two wanderers
heard cries which seemed to be uttered by a female voice. They
could not tell whether these were cries of grief or joy; however,
they instantly started up, full of that inquietude and apprehension
which a strange place naturally inspires. The cries came from two
young women who were tripping stark naked along the meadow
while two monkeys followed close at their heels, biting their backs.
Candide was moved to pity; he had learned to shoot while he was
among the Bulgarians, and he could hit a nut off a bush without
touching a leaf. Accordingly he took up his double-barrel Spanish

---

*From the Spanish *orejones*, meaning "big ears," a term used because these natives
adorned their ears with huge hanging earrings.
†The *Journal de Trévoux*, founded in 1701, was a Jesuit periodical hostile to Voltaire,
the *philosophes*, and the Enlightenment.

rifle, pulled the trigger, and killed the two monkeys. "God be praised, my dear Cacambo, I have rescued two poor creatures from a perilous situation. If I have committed a sin in killing an Inquisitor and a Jesuit, I made ample amends by saving the lives of these two distressed girls. Perhaps they are young ladies of rank, and this assistance I have been so happy to give them may gain us great advantages in this country."

He was about to continue when he felt himself struck speechless at seeing the two girls embracing the dead bodies of the monkeys in the tenderest manner, weeping over their bodies, and filling the air with the most doleful lamentations. "Really," he said to Cacambo, "I didn't expect to see so much generosity of spirit." "Master," replied the knowing valet, "you have made a precious piece of work of it: you have killed the lovers of these two ladies." "Their lovers, Cacambo! You must be joking; it cannot be; I can never believe it." "Dear sir," replied Cacambo, "you are surprised by everything; why do you think it so strange that in some countries monkeys obtain the good graces of ladies? They are one-quarter human, just as I am one-quarter Spanish." "Alas!" replied Candide, "I remember hearing my master Pangloss say that such things used to happen in former times; and that from these mixtures arose centaurs, fauns, and satyrs; and that many of the ancients had seen such monsters; but I took all that for fables." "Now you should be convinced," said Cacambo, "that it is very true; and you see what is done with those creatures by people who have not had a proper education. All I am afraid of is, that these same ladies will get us in real trouble."

These judicious reflections led Candide to leave the meadow and hide in a thicket. There he and Cacambo ate; and after heartily cursing the Grand Inquisitor, the Governor of Buenos Ayres, and the baron, they fell asleep on the ground. When they awoke, they were surprised to find that they could not move. The reason was, that the Oreillons, who inhabit that country, and to whom the ladies had given information of these two strangers, had bound them with cords made of tree bark. They saw themselves surrounded by fifty naked Oreillons, armed with bows and arrows, clubs, and hatchets of flint; some were making a fire under a large cauldron; and others were preparing spits, and all were crying out: "A Jesuit! a Jesuit!

We shall be revenged! we shall have excellent cheer; let's eat this Jesuit; let's eat him up."[18]

"I told you, master," cried Cacambo mournfully, "that these two wenches would play us a dirty trick." Candide, seeing the cauldron and the spits, cried out: "I suppose they are going to either boil or roast us. Ah! what would Pangloss say if he could see how a state of nature is formed? Everything is right. It may be so: but I must confess it seems harsh to have lost dear Miss Cunégonde, and to be spitted like a rabbit by these barbarous Oreillons." Cacambo, who never lost his presence of mind in distress, said to the disconsolate Candide: "Do not despair. I understand a little of the jargon of these people; I will speak to them." "And be sure," said Candide, "you make them aware of the horrid barbarity of boiling and roasting human creatures, and how un-Christian such a practice is."

"Gentlemen," said Cacambo, "you think perhaps you are going to feast upon a Jesuit; if so, excellent idea; nothing can be more agreeable to justice than to treat your enemies so. Indeed, the law of nature teaches us to kill our neighbour; and that's why we find this practised all over the world; and if we do not indulge ourselves in eating human flesh, it is because we have much better food; but for you, who do not have our resources, it is certainly agreed to be much better to feast upon your enemies than to throw their bodies to the crows of the air, and thus lose all the fruits of your victory. But surely, gentlemen, you will not choose to eat your friends. You imagine you are going to roast a Jesuit, but my master is your friend, your defender; and you are going to spit the very man who has been destroying your enemies. As to myself, I am your countryman; this gentleman is my master; and far from being a Jesuit, let me tell you he has just killed one of that order, whose robe he now wears, and that's why you dislike him. To prove that I'm telling the truth, take the robe he has on, and carry it to the first barrier of the Jesuits' kingdom, and ask if my master did not kill one of their officers. There will be little or no time lost by this, and you may still keep us to eat in case you find that I have lied; but, if you find that I told the truth, you are too well acquainted with the principles of the laws of society, humanity, and justice, not to let us depart unhurt."

This speech appeared very reasonable to the Oreillons. They sent

AN OREILLON RECEPTION

two of their people to inquire into the truth of this affair, who performed the task like men of sense, and soon returned with good news for our distressed adventurers. Upon this they were both freed, and those who were so recently going to roast and boil them, now showed them all sorts of civilities, offered them girls, gave them refreshments, and led them back to the border of their country, crying all the way, in token of joy: "He is no Jesuit, he is no Jesuit."

Candide could not help admiring the cause of his deliverance. "What men! what manners!" he cried; "if I had not had the good luck to run my sword up to the hilt in the body of Miss Cunégonde's brother, I would definitely have been eaten alive. But, after all, pure nature is an excellent thing; since these people, instead of eating me, showed me a thousand civilities as soon as they knew I was not a Jesuit."

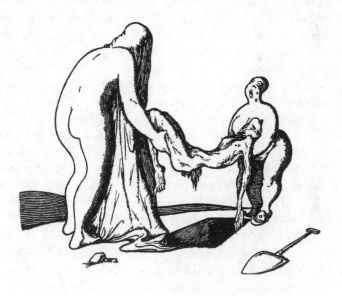

XVII

Candide and his Valet arrive in the Country of
El Dorado.* What they saw there

W hen they got to the frontier of the Oreillons, "You see,"
said Cacambo to Candide, "this hemisphere is not better
than the other; take my advice, and let's return to Europe
by the shortest possible way." "But how can we get back," said
Candide, "and where shall we go? To my own country? The Bulgarians and the Abares are slitting everyone's throat; or shall we go
to Portugal? There I will be burnt; if we stay here, we are always
in danger of being spitted. But how can I bring myself to leave that
part of the world where my dear Miss Cunégonde lives?"

"Let's go towards Cayenne," said Cacambo; "there we will meet
with some Frenchmen; for they go all over the world; perhaps they
will help and God will take pity on us."

It was not so easy to get to Cayenne. They knew roughly which
way to go; but the mountains, rivers, precipices, robbers, savages,
were dreadful obstacles in the way. Their horses died from fatigue,
and their food was gone. They subsisted a whole month on wild
fruit, till at length they came to a little river bordered with cocoa
trees, the sight of which at once revived their drooping spirits, and
supplied nourishment for their enfeebled bodies.

Cacambo, who was always giving as good advice as the old
woman herself, said to Candide: "You see there is no holding out
any longer; we have travelled enough on foot. I see an empty canoe
near the river-side; let's fill it with cocoa-nuts, get into it and float
with the current: a river always leads to some inhabited place. If we
do not meet with agreeable things, we shall at least meet with some-

---

*Literally, "golden country" (Spanish); a mythical utopian society, with origins in
travel accounts of the New World, that had great appeal for Europeans.

thing new." "Agreed," cried Candide; "let's let Providence guide us."

They rowed a few leagues down the river, the banks of which in some places were covered with flowers, in others barren; in some parts smooth and level, and in others steep and rugged. The stream widened as they went farther on, till at length it passed under one of the frightful rocks whose summits seemed to reach the clouds. Here our two travellers had the courage to commit themselves to the stream, which, narrowing at this point, hurried them along with a dreadful noise and speed. At the end of twenty-four hours they saw daylight again; but their canoe was smashed to pieces against the rocks. They had to creep along from rock to rock for the length of one league, till at length a spacious plain came into sight. This place was ringed by a chain of inaccessible mountains. The country appeared cultivated for pleasure as well as to produce the necessaries of life. The useful was joined to the agreeable. The roads were covered, or rather adorned, with carriages formed of glittering materials, in which were men and women of surprising beauty, drawn with great speed by red sheep of a very large size, which far surpassed the finest horses of Andalusia, Tetuan, or Mecquinez.

"Here is a country," said Candide, "that's better than Westphalia." He and Cacambo landed near the first village they saw, at the entrance of which they noticed some children, covered with tattered garments of the richest brocade, playing quoits. Our two inhabitants of the other hemisphere amused themselves greatly with what they saw. The quoits were large round pieces, yellow, red, and green, which cast a most glorious lustre. Our travellers picked some of them up, and they proved to be gold, emeralds, rubies and diamonds the least of which would have been the greatest ornament to the superb throne of the Great Mogul. "Without doubt," said Cacambo, "those children who are playing quoits must be the king's sons." As he was uttering these words the schoolmaster of the village appeared, to call them back to school. "There," said Candide, "is the tutor of the royal family."

The little ragamuffins immediately dropped their game, leaving the quoits on the ground with all their other playthings. Candide gathered them up, ran to the schoolmaster, and, with a most respectful bow, presented them to him, giving him to understand by signs, that their royal highnesses had forgotten their gold and precious stones. The schoolmaster, with a smile, flung them upon the ground; then examining Candide from head to foot with an air of admiration, he turned his back and went on his way.

Our travellers took care, however, to gather up the gold, the rubies and the emeralds. "Where are we?" cried Candide: "The king's children in this country must have an excellent education, since they are taught to show such a contempt for gold and precious stones." Cacambo was as much surprised as his master. At last they came to the first house in the village, which was built in the manner of a European palace. There was a crowd of people around the door, and a still greater number in the house. The sound of the most delightful instruments of music was heard, and a delicious aroma came from the kitchen. Cacambo went up to the door and heard those within talking in Peruvian, which was his mother tongue; for Cacambo was born in the village of Tucuman, where no other language is spoken. "I will be your interpreter here," he said to Candide "let's go in; this is an eating-house."

Immediately two waiters and two servant-girls, dressed in cloth of gold, and with their hair braided with ribbons, invited them to sit down at the table. The dinner consisted of four dishes of different soups, each garnished with two young parakeets, a large dish of bouille that weighed two hundred pounds, two roasted monkeys of a delicious flavour, three hundred humming-birds in one dish, and six hundred fly-birds in another; some excellent ragouts, delicate tarts, and the whole thing served up in dishes of rock-crystal. Several sorts of liquors, extracted from sugar-cane, were handed about by the servants who attended.

Most of the company were merchants and waggoners, all extremely polite; they asked Cacambo a few questions with the utmost discretion and circumspection; and replied to him in a most obliging and satisfactory manner.

As soon as dinner was over, both Candide and Cacambo thought they could pay very handsomely for their entertainment by laying down two of those large gold pieces which they had picked off the ground; but the landlord and landlady burst into a fit of laughing and held their sides for some time. When the fit was over: "Gentlemen," said the landlord, "I clearly see that you are strangers. We are not accustomed to meeting foreigners; therefore pardon us for laughing when you offered us the common pebbles of our highways in payment for your dinner. No doubt, you don't have any of our currency; but there is no need for any money at all to dine in this house. All the inns, which are established for the convenience of those who carry on the trade of this nation, are maintained by the government. You have found but very meager entertainment here, because this is only a poor village; but in almost every other of these public-houses you will be given a reception worthy of your merit." Cacambo explained the whole of this speech of the landlord to Candide, who listened to it with the same astonishment with which his friend communicated it. "What sort of a country is this," said the one to the other "that is unknown to all the world, and where nature itself is so different from our own? Possibly this is that part of the globe where everything is right, for there must certainly be some such place. And for all that Master Pangloss said on the matter, I often perceived that things went very badly in Westphalia."

XVIII

What they saw in the Country of El Dorado

Cacambo revealed all his curiosity to his host with a thousand different questions: the honest man answered him thus: "I am very ignorant, sir, but I am contented with my ignorance; however, we have in this neighbourhood an old man retired from Court, who is the most learned and communicative person in the kingdom." He then brought Cacambo to the old man; Candide acted now only a secondary character, and attended his own valet. They entered a very plain house, for the door was nothing but silver, and the ceiling was only of beaten gold, but wrought in so elegant a taste as to vie with the richest. The ante-chamber, indeed, was only decorated with rubies and emeralds; but the order in which everything was arranged made amends for this great simplicity.

The old man received the strangers on his sofa, which was stuffed with humming-birds' feathers, and ordered his servants to present them with liquors in golden goblets; after which he satisfied their curiosity in the following terms:

"I am now one hundred and seventy-two years old; and I heard from my late father, who was liveryman to the king, the amazing revolutions of Peru which he had seen. This kingdom is the ancient country of the Incas, who very imprudently left it to conquer another part of the world, and were ultimately conquered and destroyed themselves by the Spaniards.

"Those princes of their family who remained in their native country acted more wisely. They decreed, with the consent of their whole nation, that none of the inhabitants of our little kingdom should ever leave it; and to this wise rule we owe the preservation of our innocence and happiness. The Spaniards had some confused notion of this country, to which they gave the name El Dorado; and

Sir Walter Raleigh,* an Englishman, actually came very near it about three hundred years ago; but the inaccessible rocks and precipices with which our country is surrounded on all sides, has protected us so far from the rapacious fury of the people of Europe, who have an unaccountable fondness for the pebbles and dirt of our land, for the sake of which they would murder us all to the very last man."

The conversation lasted some time, and addressed the form of government, their manners, their women, their public diversions, and the arts. At length, Candide, who had always had a taste for metaphysics, asked whether the people of that country had any religion.

The old man reddened a little at this question. "Can you doubt it?" he said. "Do you take us for wretches who have no sense of gratitude?" Cacambo asked in a respectful manner about the established religion of El Dorado. The old man blushed again, and said: "Can there be two religions then? Ours, I suppose, is the religion of the whole world. We worship God from morning till night." "Do you worship only one God?" said Cacambo, who still acted as interpreter of Candide's doubts. "Certainly," said the old man; "there are not two nor three nor four Gods. I must confess the people of your world ask very extraordinary questions." However, Candide could not refrain from making many more inquiries of the old man. He wanted to know how they prayed to God in El Dorado. "We do not pray to him at all," said the reverend sage. "We have nothing to ask of him. He has given us all we want, and we give him thanks continually." Candide was interested in seeing some of their priests and had Cacambo ask the old man where they were; at which he, smiling, said: "My friends, we are all priests. The king and all the heads of families sing solemn hymns of thanksgiving every morning, accompanied by five or six thousand musicians." "What!" says Cacambo, "you have no monks among you to dispute, to govern, to intrigue, and to burn people who are not of the same opinion as themselves?" "Do you take us for fools?" said the old man; "here we are all of one opinion, and don't know what you're

---

*English soldier and explorer (1554?–1618).

up to with your monks." During this whole discourse Candide was overjoyed, and he said to himself: "What a massive difference there is between this place and Westphalia, and this house and the baron's castle! Ah, Master Pangloss! if you could have seen El Dorado you would no longer have maintained that the castle of Thunder-ten-tronckh was the finest of all possible edifices. There is nothing like seeing the world, that's certain."

After this long conversation, the old man ordered six sheep to be harnessed and put to the coach, and sent twelve of his servants to escort the travellers to Court. "Excuse me," he said, "for not accompanying you; my age deprives me of that honour. The king will receive you in such a manner that you will have no reason to complain; and doubtless you will make allowance for the customs of the country if there happen to be any that displease you."

Candide and Cacambo got into the coach, the six sheep flew, and in less than a quarter of an hour they arrived at the king's palace, which was situated at the far end of the capital. At the entrance was a portal two hundred and twenty feet high, and one hundred wide; but it is impossible for words to describe the materials of the entryway. The reader can imagine how much finer it was than the pebbles and sand which we call gold and precious stones.

Twenty beautiful young virgins in waiting welcomed Candide and Cacambo as they stepped from the coach, led them to the bath, and dressed them in robes made of the down of humming-birds; afterwards they were introduced by the great officers of the crown, both male and female, to the king's apartment, between two files of musicians, each file consisting of a thousand, as is customary in that country. When they drew near to the throne room, Cacambo asked one of the officers how they were to pay their respects to his majesty; whether it was the custom to fall upon their knees, or to prostrate themselves upon the ground? whether they should put their hands on their heads or behind their backs? whether they should lick the dust off the floor? in short, what was the proper form for such occasions? "The custom," said the great officer, "is to embrace the king, and kiss him on each cheek." Candide and Cacambo threw their arms around his majesty's neck, who received them in the most gracious manner imaginable, and very politely asked them to dine with him.

While supper was being prepared, orders were given to show them the city, where they saw public buildings that rose to the clouds; the market-places decorated with a thousand columns; fountains of spring water, and others of rose-water, and of liquors drawn from sugar-cane, incessantly flowing in the great squares, which were paved with a kind of precious stone that emitted an odour like that of cloves and cinnamon. Candide asked to see the High Court of Justice, the Parliament; but was told that none existed in that country, that lawsuits were unknown. He then asked if they had any prisons; they replied, none. But what gave him the greatest surprise and pleasure was the Palace of Sciences, where he saw a gallery, two thousand feet long, filled with the various instruments of mathematics and natural philosophy.

After having spent the whole afternoon seeing only one-thousandth of the city, they were brought back to the king's palace. Candide sat down at the table with his majesty, his valet Cacambo, and several ladies of the court. Never was entertainment more elegant, nor could anyone possibly show more wit than his majesty displayed while they were at supper. Cacambo explained all the king's *bon mots* to Candide, and although they were translated, they still appeared to be *bon mots*. Of all the things that surprised Candide, this was not the least astonishing. They spent a whole month in this hospitable place, during which time Candide was continually saying to Cacambo, "I admit, my friend, once more that the castle where I was born is a mere nothing in comparison with the place where we now are; but still Miss Cunégonde is not here, and you yourself probably have some fair one in Europe for whom you sigh. If we stay here we will be just like everyone else; but if we return to our own world with only a dozen El Dorado sheep loaded with the pebbles of this country, we shall be richer than all the kings in Europe; we will no longer need to fear the inquisitors; and we may easily recover Miss Cunégonde."

This speech was perfectly agreeable to Cacambo. A fondness for roving, for making a name for themselves in their own country, and for boasting of what they had seen in their travels, was so strong in our two wanderers, that they resolved to be no longer happy; and demanded permission of the king to leave the country.

"You are about to do a rash and silly thing," said the king. "I know that my kingdom is an insignificant spot; but when people are tolerably at ease in a place, I'd think it would be to their interest to remain there. Most assuredly I have no right to detain you or any strangers against your wills: that sort of tyranny is repugnant to our manners and our laws: all men are by nature free; you have therefore the liberty to depart whenever you please, but you will encounter many great difficulties in crossing the frontiers. It is impossible to travel up that rapid river which runs under high and vaulted rocks, and by which you were conveyed here by a kind of miracle. The mountains by which my kingdom are hemmed in on all sides, are ten thousand feet high, and perfectly perpendicular; each one is more than ten leagues across, and the only way down is over precipices. However, since you are determined to leave us, I will immediately give orders to the superintendent of my carriages to have one made that will carry you safely. When they have taken you to the back of the mountains, nobody will be able to go with you farther; for my subjects have made a vow never to leave the kingdom, and they are too prudent to break it. Ask me whatever else you please." "All we shall ask of your majesty," said Cacambo, "is only a few sheep laden with provisions, pebbles, and the clay of your country." The king smiled at the request, and said: "I cannot imagine what pleasure you Europeans find in our yellow clay; but take away as much of it as you will, and may it do you much good."

He immediately gave orders to his engineers to make a machine to hoist these two extraordinary men out of the kingdom. Three thousand good mathematicians went to work and finished it in about fifteen days; and it did not cost more than twenty millions sterling of that country's money. Candide and Cacambo were placed on this machine, and they took with them two large red sheep, bridled and saddled, to ride upon when they got on the other side of the mountains; twenty others for carrying provisions; thirty laden with presents of the rareties of that country; and fifty with gold, diamonds and other precious stones. The king at parting with our two adventurers, embraced them with the greatest cordiality.

He made a fine spectacle, the manner of their setting off, and the ingenious method by which they and their sheep were hoisted to the top of the mountains. The mathematicians and engineers left them as soon as they had conveyed them to a place of safety; and

Candide was wholly occupied with the thoughts of presenting his sheep to Miss Cunégonde. "Now," said he, "thanks to Heaven, we have more than enough to pay the Governor of Buenos Ayres for Miss Cunégonde, if indeed a price can be placed on her. Let's make the best of our way to Cayenne, where we will take a ship, and then we may at leisure think of what kingdom we shall purchase with our riches."

XIX

What happened to them at Surinam, and how
Candide got to know Martin*

Our travellers' first day's journey was very pleasant; they
were elated with the prospect of possessing more riches
than were to be found in Europe, Asia, and Africa together.
Candide, in an amorous mood, cut the name of Miss Cunégonde
on almost every tree he came to. The second day, two of their sheep
sank in a swamp, and were swallowed up, with their loads; two
more died of fatigue; some few days afterward seven or eight perished with hunger in a desert; and others, at different times, tumbled down precipices, or were otherwise lost; so that, after travelling
about a hundred days, they had only two sheep left of the hundred
and two they brought with them from El Dorado. Candide said to
Cacambo: "You see, my dear friend, how fleeting the riches of this
world are; there is nothing solid but virtue." "Very true," said Cacambo; "but we still have two sheep remaining, with more treasure
than the King of Spain will ever have; and I see a town at a distance,
which I take to be Surinam, a town belonging to the Dutch. We are
now at the end of our troubles, and at the beginning of happiness."

As they approached the town, they saw a negro stretched on the
ground with only half of his outfit, which was a kind of linen frock,
for the poor man had lost his left leg and his right hand. "Good
God," said Candide in Dutch; "what are you doing in this horrible
condition?" "I am waiting for my master, Mynheer† Vanderdendur,
the famous trader," answered the negro. "Was it Mynheer Vanderdendur who used you in this cruel manner?" "Yes, sir," said the
negro; "it is the custom here. They give us a linen garment twice

---

*Dutch colony in South America.
† "My master" or "Sir" (Dutch).

a year, and that is all. When we work in the sugar factory, and the mill happens to snatch off a finger, they instantly chop off our hand; and when we attempt to run away they cut off a leg.* Both these things have happened to me; and it is at this cost that you eat sugar in Europe;† and yet when my mother sold me for ten Patagonian crowns on the coast of Guinea, she said to me: 'My dear child, bless our fetishes; adore them for ever; they will make you happy; you have the honour to be a slave to our lords the whites, by which you will make the fortune of your parents. Alas! I don't know if I have made their fortunes; but they have not made mine. Dogs, monkeys, and parrots are a thousand times less wretched than I. The Dutch fetishists who converted me tell me every Sunday that the blacks and whites are all children of one father, whom they call Adam. I'm no genealogist; but if what these preachers say is true, we are all second cousins; and you must admit that no one could treat his own relations in a more horrible manner."

"O Pangloss!" cried out Candide, "such horrid doings never entered your imagination. Here is an end of the matter; I find myself, after all, obliged to renounce your optimism." "Optimism," said Cacambo, "what is that?" "Alas!" replied Candide, "it is the obstinacy of maintaining that everything is best when it is worst"; and so saying, he turned his eyes towards the poor negro, and shed a flood of tears; and in this weeping mood he entered the town of Surinam.

Immediately upon their arrival our travellers asked if there was any ship in the harbour which could be sent to Buenos Ayres. The person they asked happened to be the master of a Spanish boat, who offered to make a fair bargain with them and arranged for them to meet at a café. Candide and his faithful Cacambo went to wait for him there, taking with them their two sheep.

Candide, who was all frankness and sincerity, gave an ingenious retelling of his adventures to the Spaniard, and he confessed that he wanted to recapture Miss Cunégonde from the Governor of Buenos Ayres. "Oh, oh!" said the shipmaster, "if that is the case get someone else to carry you to Buenos Ayres; for my part, I wash my

---

*This description of the cruel mistreatment of slaves is based on historical fact.
†Scathing reference to a colonial system that placed profit above humane values.

hands of the affair. I would be hanged and so would you. The fair Cunégonde is the Governor's favourite mistress." These words were like a clap of thunder to Candide; he wept bitterly for a long time, and taking Cacambo aside, he said: "I'll tell you, my dear friend, what you must do. We each have in our pockets five or six millions in diamonds; you are cleverer at these matters than I; you must go to Buenos Ayres and bring back Miss Cunégonde. If the Governor gives you any difficulty, give him a million; if he holds out, give him two; you have not killed an Inquisitor, no one will suspect you: I'll outfit another ship and go to Venice, where I will wait for you. Venice is a free country, where we will have nothing to fear from Bulgarians, Abares, Jews, or Inquisitors." Cacambo greatly applauded this wise plan. He was in despair at the thought of parting with so good a master, who treated him more like an intimate friend than a servant; but the pleasure of being able to do him a service soon got the better of his sorrow. They embraced each other amid a flood of tears. Candide urged him not to forget the old woman. Cacambo set out the same day. This Cacambo was a very honest fellow.

Candide continued some days longer at Surinam, waiting for any captain to carry him and his two remaining sheep to Italy. He hired domestics, and purchased many things necessary for the long voyage; finally, Mynheer Vanderdendur, skipper of a large Dutch vessel, came and offered his service. "What will you charge," said Candide, "to carry me, my servants, my baggage, and these two sheep you see here, directly to Venice?" The skipper asked for ten thousand piastres; and Candide agreed to his demand without hesitation.

"Ho, ho!" said the cunning Vanderdendur to himself, "this stranger must be very rich; he agrees to give me ten thousand piastres without hesitation." Returning a little while later, he told Candide that, upon second consideration he could not undertake the voyage for less than twenty thousand. "Very well, you shall have them," said Candide.

"Well!" said the skipper to himself, "this man agrees to pay twenty thousand piastres with as much ease as ten." So he went back again to say that he will not carry him to Venice for less than thirty thousand piastres. "Then you shall have thirty thousand," said Candide.

"Ah ha!" said the Dutchman once more to himself, "thirty thousand piastres mean nothing to this man. Those sheep must certainly be laden with an immense treasure. I'll stop here and ask no more; but make him pay up front the thirty thousand piastres, and then we'll see." Candide sold two small diamonds, the least of which was worth more than all the skipper asked. He paid him in advance; the two sheep were put on board, and Candide followed in a small boat to join the vessel at its anchorage. The skipper took his opportunity, hoisted sail, and put out to sea with a favourable wind. Candide, confounded and amazed, soon lost sight of the ship. "Alas!" said he, "this is a trick worthy of our old world!" He returned back to the shore overwhelmed with grief; and indeed he had lost what would have made the fortune of twenty monarchs.

Immediately upon his landing he applied to the Dutch magistrate. Because he was feeling troubled, he thundered at the door, went in, made his case, and talked a little louder than was necessary. The magistrate began by fining him ten thousand piastres for making such a racket, and then listened very patiently to what he had to say; promised to look into the affair on the skipper's return; and ordered him to pay ten thousand piastres more for the fees of the court.

This treatment completed Candide's despair. It is true he had suffered misfortunes a thousand times more grievous; but the cool insolence of the judge and the villainy of the skipper raised his anger and threw him into a deep melancholy. The villainy of mankind presented itself to his mind in all its deformity, and his mind dwelt only on gloomy thoughts. After some time, hearing that the captain of a French ship was ready to set sail for Bordeaux, as he had no more sheep loaded with diamonds to put on board, he took a cabin at a fair price; and made it known in the town that he would pay the passage and board of any honest man who would keep him company during the voyage, besides making him a present of ten thousand piastres, on condition that such person must be the most disgusted with his own condition, and the most unhappy in the whole province.

This drew such a crowd of candidates that a large fleet could not have contained them. Candide, willing to choose among those who appeared most likely to answer his intention, selected twenty, who seemed to him the most companionable, and who all pretended to be more miserable than all the others. He invited them to his inn, and promised to treat them to supper, on condition that every man would swear to tell his own history; declaring at the same time that he would select that person who appeared to him the most deserving of compassion and the most truly dissatisfied with his condition of life, and that he would distribute various gifts among the rest.

This extraordinary assembly continued sitting till four in the morning. Candide, while he was listening to their adventures, recalled what the old woman had said to him during their voyage to Buenos Ayres, and the bet she had made that there was not a person on board the ship who had not met with some great misfortunes. Every story he heard made him think of Pangloss. "My old master," said he, "would be hard pressed to prove his system. If only he were here! Certainly, if everything is for the best, it is in El Dorado, and not in the other parts of the world." Finally he selected a poor scholar, who had worked ten years for the booksellers at Amsterdam. He decided that no employment could be more detestable.

This scholar, who was in fact a very honest man, had been robbed by his wife, beaten by his son, and forsaken by his daughter, who had run away with a Portuguese. He had also been fired from the little job on which he existed, and he was persecuted by the clergy of Surinam, who took him for a Socinian.[19] It must be acknowledged that the other competitors were at least as wretched as he. But Candide hoped that the company of a man of letters would relieve the tediousness of the voyage. All the other candidates complained that Candide had done them great injustice, but he pacified them with a present of a hundred piastres to each.

XX

What happened to Candide and Martin at sea

The old philosopher, whose name was Martin, set sail with Candide for Bordeaux. They both had seen and suffered a great deal; and even if the ship had been sailing from Surinam to Japan round the Cape of Good Hope, they would have been able to keep themselves amused during the whole voyage with instances of moral and natural evil.

Candide, however, had one advantage over Martin; he still hoped to see Miss Cunégonde once more, whereas the poor philosopher had nothing to hope for; besides, Candide had money and jewels, and though he had lost a hundred red sheep laden with the greatest treasure on earth, and though he still had in his heart the memory of the Dutch skipper's villainy, yet when he considered what he had still left, and repeated the name of Cunégonde, especially after meal times, he leaned toward Pangloss's doctrine.

"And," said he to Martin, "what is your opinion of this system? What is your idea of moral and natural evil?" "Sir," replied Martin, "our priest accused me of being a Socinian: but the real truth is, I am a Manichæan."[20] "You're joking," said Candide, "there aren't any more Manichæans in the world." "And yet I am one," said Martin; "but I cannot help it; I cannot think otherwise." "Surely the devil must be in you," said Candide. "He is mixed up with so many," replied Martin, "of the affairs of this world, that it is very probable he may be in me as well as everywhere else; but I must confess, when I cast my eye on this globe, or rather globule, I cannot help thinking that God has abandoned it to some evil being—all of it except El Dorado. I have scarcely seen a city that did not wish the destruction of its neighbouring city, nor a family that did not desire to exterminate some other family. The poor in all parts of the world bear an inveterate hatred against the rich, even while they creep and cringe to them; and the rich treat the poor like sheep, whose wool and flesh they barter for money: a million regimented assassins roam Europe from one end to the other, carrying out murder and robbery with such discipline in order to earn their bread because there is no more honest profession for them. Even in those cities which seem to enjoy the blessings of peace, and where the arts flourish, the inhabitants are devoured by envy, cares and anxieties, which are greater plagues than any experienced in a town when it is under siege. Private griefs are still more dreadful than public calamities. In a word," concluded the philosopher, "I have seen and suffered so much that I am a Manichæan."

"And yet there is some good in the world," replied Candide. "Maybe so," said Martin; "but it has escaped my knowledge."

While they were deeply engaged in this dispute they heard the rumble of cannon, which grew louder every moment. Each took out his spy-glass, and they saw two ships fighting at the distance of about three miles away. The wind brought them both so near the French ship that they had the pleasure of seeing the fight with great ease. After several smart broadsides, the one gave the other a shot so well aimed that it sank her outright. Then Candide and Martin could easily see a hundred men on the deck of the vessel which was sinking, who, with hands raised to heaven, sent forth piercing cries and were in a moment swallowed up by the waves.

"Well," said Martin, "you now see how mankind treat each other." "It is certain," said Candide, "that there is something diabolical in this affair." As he was speaking, he noticed something of a shining red hue, floating close to the sunken vessel. They sent a boat to investigate what it might be, and it proved to be one of his sheep. Candide felt more joy at the recovery of this one animal than he did grief when he lost the other hundred, all laden with the large diamonds of El Dorado.

The French captain quickly realized that the victorious ship belonged to the crown of Spain; that the other was a Dutch pirate and the very same captain who had robbed Candide. The immense riches which this villain had stolen were buried with him in the sea, and only this one sheep was saved. "You see," said Candide to Martin, "that vice is sometimes punished; this villain the Dutch skipper has met with the fate he deserves." "Very true," said Martin "but why should the passengers perish too? God has punished the knave, and the devil has drowned the rest."

The French and Spanish ships continued on their journey, and Candide and Martin continued their conversation. They disputed for fifteen days in a row and at the end of that time they were just as far advanced as the first moment they began. However, they had the satisfaction of talking, of communicating their ideas, and of comforting each other. Candide embraced his sheep: "Since I have found you again," said he, "I may possibly find my Cunégonde once more."

XXI

Candide and Martin draw near to the coast of France. They reason with each other

They could finally see the coast of France, when Candide said to Martin: "Mr Martin, were you ever in France?" "Yes, sir," said Martin, "I have been in several provinces of that kingdom. In some half of the people are fools and madmen; in some they are too sly; in still others they are in general either very good-natured or very brutal; while in others they affect to be witty; and in all their ruling passion is love, the next is slander, and the last is to talk nonsense." "But, Mr Martin, were you ever in Paris?" "Yes, sir, I have been in that city, and it is a place that contains all species just described. It is a chaos, a confused multitude, where every one seeks pleasure without being able to find it: at least, as far as I have observed during my short stay in that city. At my arrival I was robbed of everything I had by pickpockets at the fair of St. Germain.* I myself was taken for a robber, and confined in prison a whole week, after which I took a job as a proofreader, in order to get enough money to return on foot to Holland. I knew the whole tribe of scribblers, malcontents and fanatics. It is said that the people of that city are very polite: I believe they may be so."

"I myself have no curiosity to see France," said Candide. "You no doubt realize that after spending a month at El Dorado, I desire to see nothing but Miss Cunégonde; I am going to wait for her at Venice. I intend to pass through France on my way to Italy; will you not accompany me?" "With all my heart," said Martin. "They say Venice is good only for noble Venetians, but that, nevertheless, strangers are well treated there when they have plenty of money. Now I have none, but you have; therefore I will follow you any-

---

*Street fair held on the left bank of the Seine, in a quarter of Paris near the old church of Saint-Germain-des-Prés.

where." "By the way," said Candide, "do you think that the earth was originally sea, as we read in that great book* which belongs to the captain of the ship?" "I don't believe any of that," replied Martin, "any more than I do of the many other chimeras which people have been peddling for some time past." "But then why," said Candide, "was the world formed?" "To drive us mad," said Martin. "Aren't you surprised," continued Candide, "at the love which the two girls in the country of the Oreillons had for those two monkeys? You know I have told you the story." "Surprised!" replied Martin, "not in the least; I see nothing strange in this passion. I have seen so many extraordinary things that there is nothing extraordinary to me now." "Do you think," said Candide, "that mankind always massacred each other as they do now? Were they always guilty of lies, fraud, treachery, ingratitude, inconstancy, envy, ambition, and cruelty? Were they always thieves, fools, cowards, gluttons, drunkards, misers, calumniators, debauchees, fanatics and hypocrites?" "Do you believe," said Martin, "that hawks have always eaten pigeons when they could get them?" "Of course," said Candide. "Well, then," replied Martin, "if hawks have always had the same nature, why do you suppose that mankind has changed?" "Oh!" said Candide, "there is a great deal of difference; because free will——" And disputing in this manner they arrived at Bordeaux.

---

*The Bible.

XXII

What happened to Candide and Martin in France

Candide stayed at Bordeaux only long enough to sell a few of the pebbles he had brought from El Dorado, and to provide himself with a carriage for two persons, for he could no longer do without his philosopher Martin. The only thing that upset him was having to part with his sheep, which he entrusted to the care of the Academy of Sciences at Bordeaux, who proposed, as a theme for that year's prize contest, to prove why the wool of this sheep was red; and the prize was awarded to a northern sage, who demonstrated by A plus B minus C, divided by Z, why the sheep must necessarily be red, and die of the mange.*

In the meantime, all the travellers whom Candide met with in the inns or on the road told him that they were going to Paris. This general eagerness gave him likewise a great desire to see this capital, and it was not much out of his way to Venice.

He entered the city by the suburbs of St. Marceau,† and thought he was in one of the vilest villages in all Westphalia.

Candide had not been long at his inn before he came down with a mild illness caused by exhaustion. As he wore a diamond of an enormous size on his finger, and people had noticed among the rest of his luggage a safe that seemed very heavy, he soon found himself between two physicians whom he had not sent for, a number of intimate friends whom he had never seen and who would not leave his bedside, and two pious ladies, who warmed his broth.

"I remember," said Martin to him, "that the first time I came to

---

*Contagious disease of domestic and wild animals; also known as red mange and sheep pox.

†Poor, populous, and unattractive quarter of Paris, on the left bank of the Seine.

Paris I also got sick. I was very poor, and consequently I had neither friends, nurses, nor physicians, and yet I did very well."

However, as a result of the purging and bleeding,* Candide's condition became very serious. The priest of the parish came with all imaginable politeness to ask for a note payable to the bearer in the other world.† Candide refused to comply with his request, but the two pious ladies assured him that it was a new fashion. Candide replied that he was not one to follow fashion. Martin wanted to throw the priest out of the window. The cleric swore that Candide would not have Christian burial. Martin swore in his turn that he would bury the cleric alive if he continued to bother them any longer. The dispute grew heated; Martin took him by the shoulders and turned him out of the room, which caused a great scandal and developed into a legal case.

Candide recovered, and till he was in a condition to go abroad, he had a great deal of very good company to pass the evenings with him in his chamber. They played cards. Candide was surprised to find he could never turn a trick, and Martin was not at all surprised.

Among those who did him the honours of the place was a little spruce Abbé of Perigord—one of those insinuating, busy, fawning, impudent, necessary fellows, who waylay passing strangers, tell them all the scandal of the town, and offer to see to their pleasures at any price. This man conducted Candide and Martin to the play-house: they were performing a new tragedy. Candide found himself seated near a cluster of wits. This, however, did not prevent him from shedding tears at some scenes, which were most affecting and well acted. One of these talkers said to him between the acts: "You are quite mistaken to shed tears. That actress is horrible, and the man who acts with her still worse, and the play itself is more execrable than the actors in it. The author does not understand a word of Arabic, and yet he has set his scene in Arabia; and what is more, he is a man who does not believe in innate ideas. To-morrow I will bring you a score of pamphlets that have been written against him."

---

*Ironical reference to medical remedies that had become old-fashioned by the middle of the eighteenth century.
†Beginning in 1750 *billets de confessions* were required of dying patients on pain of refusal of the sacraments and absolution.

"Tell me, sir," said Candide to the Abbé, "how many plays are there for performance in France?" "Five or six thousand," replied the other. "Indeed! that is a great number," said Candide; "but how many good ones are there?" "About fifteen or sixteen." "Oh! that is a great number," said Martin.

Candide was greatly taken with an actress who performed the part of Queen Elizabeth in a rather dull tragedy.* "That actress," he said to Martin, "pleases me greatly. She has some resemblance to Miss Cunégonde. I would like to meet her." The Abbé of Perigord offered to introduce him to her at her own house. Candide, who was brought up in Germany, wanted to know how one behaved in France with Queens of England. "There is a necessary distinction to be observed in these matters," said the Abbé. "In a country town we take them to a tavern; here in Paris they are treated with great respect during their lifetime, while they are attractive, and when they die we throw their bodies upon a dunghill."[21] "How," said Candide, "throw a Queen's body upon a dunghill!" "The gentleman is quite right," said Martin; "he tells you nothing but the truth. I happened to be in Paris when Miss Monimia made her exit, as one may say, out of this world into another. She was refused what they call here the rites of sepulture; that is to say she was denied the privilege of rotting in a churchyard by the side of all the beggars in the parish.[22] They buried her at the corner of Burgundy Street, which must certainly have shocked her, for she had very exalted notions of things." "That was very rude," said Candide. "Lord!" said Martin, "what do you expect? It is the way of these people. Imagine all the contradictions, all the inconsistencies possible, and you may meet with them in the government, the courts of justice, the churches, and the public spectacles of this odd nation." "Is it true," said Candide, "that the people of Paris are always laughing?" "Yes," replied the Abbé; "but it is with anger in their hearts. They express all their complaints by loud bursts of laughter, and commit the most detestable crimes with a smile on their faces."

"Who was that great overgrown beast," said Candide, "who

---

*Reference to *Le Comte d'Essex*, a tragedy by Thomas Corneille (1625–1709), brother of the more successful Pierre Corneille (1606–1684), who is considered a master of French tragedy.

THE ILLNESS OF CANDIDE IN PARIS

spoke so nastily to me about the play over which I was weeping, and about the actors who gave me so much pleasure?" "A very good-for-nothing sort of a man, I assure you," answered the Abbé; "one who gets his livelihood by slandering every new book and play that is written or performed. He hates to see any one meet with success, like eunuchs, who detest every one who possesses those powers they are deprived of. He is one of those vipers in literature who nourish themselves with their own venom; a pamphlet-monger." "A pamphlet-monger?" said Candide; "what is that?" "Why, a pamphlet-monger," replied the Abbé, "is a writer of pamphlets, a fool."

Candide, Martin, and the Abbé of Perigord argued on the staircase while they watched the crowd leaving the theater. "Though I am in a great hurry to see Miss Cunégonde again," said Candide, "I also have a great inclination to dine with Miss Clairon, for I am really much taken with her."

The Abbé was not the person to approach this lady's house, which was frequented by none but the best company. "She is engaged this evening," said he; "but I will have the honour of introducing you to a lady of quality of my acquaintance, at whose house you will see as much of the manners of Paris as if you had lived there for forty years."

Candide, who was naturally curious, allowed himself to be taken to this lady's house, which was in the suburbs of St Honoré.* The people gathered there were playing a game of basset;† twelve melancholy gamblers held each in his hand a small pack of cards, the corners of which, turned down, were the summaries of their bad luck. A profound silence reigned through the assembly, the gamblers were pallid and the banker was uneasy; and the lady of the house, who was seated next to him, observed with lynx's eyes every parole‡ and bet at long odds which the players signaled by folding the corners of the cards, and she made them unfold their cards with

---

*Fashionable quarter of Paris on the right bank of the Seine.

†Better known as faro; a card game, played with fifty-two cards, in which the players bet on the cards to be turned up from the top of the dealer's pack.

‡An indication that there was cheating; a "paroli" is an illegal doubling of one's bet.

a severe exactness, though mixed with a politeness, lest she frighten away her customers. This lady assumed the title of Marchioness of Parolignac. Her daughter, a girl of about fifteen years of age, was one of the gamblers, and tipped off her mamma, by signs, when any one of the players attempted to undo their ill-fortune by a little innocent deception. This is how the group was occupied when Candide, Martin and the Abbé made their entrance. Not a creature rose to salute them, or indeed took the least notice of them, being instead completely absorbed with their cards. "Ah!" said Candide, "My lady Baroness of Thunder-ten-tronckh would have behaved more civilly."

However, the Abbé whispered in the ear of the Marchioness, who, half raising herself from her seat, honoured Candide with a gracious smile, and gave Martin a nod of her head with an air of inexpressible dignity. She then gave a seat and dealt some cards to Candide, who lost fifty thousand francs in two rounds; after this they ate very elegantly, and every one was surprised at seeing Candide lose so much money without appearing to be upset over it. The servants in waiting said to each other, "This is certainly some English lord."

The supper was like most others of this kind in Paris. At first every one was silent; then followed a few confused murmurs, and afterwards several insipid jokes, false reports, false reasonings, a little politics, and a great deal of scandal. The conversation then turned upon the new productions in literature. "Tell me," said the Abbé, "have you seen the romance written by the Sieur Gauchat, doctor of divinity?"* "Yes," answered one of the guests, "but I didn't have patience to finish it. The town is pestered with a swarm of impertinent publications, but this of Dr Gauchat's outdoes them all. In short, I was so horribly tired of reading this vile stuff, that I even decided to come here, and play cards." "But what do you think about the Archdeacon T——'s† miscellaneous collection?" said the Abbé. "Oh, my God!" cried the Marchioness of Parolignac, "never mention that tedious creature. He takes such pains to tell you what everyone knows; and how he talks so learnedly on matters that are

---

*Gabriel Gauchat, a contemporary critic hostile to Voltaire and the Encyclopedists.
†Nicholas-Charles-Joseph Trublet, editor of the *Journal Chrétien*, and another enemy of Voltaire.

hardly worth the slightest consideration! How absurdly he makes use of other people's wit! how miserably he mangles what he has pilfered from them! The man makes me quite sick. A few pages of the good archdeacon are plenty."

There was at the table a person of learning and taste, who supported what the Marchioness had said. They next began to talk of tragedies. The lady wanted to know why there were several tragedies which still continued to be performed, though they were unreadable. The man of taste explained very clearly, how a play might have a certain interest without having a grain of merit. He showed, in a few words, that it is not enough to throw together a few incidents that can be found in every novel, and that dazzle the spectator; the thoughts should be new without being far-fetched; frequently sublime, but always natural; the author should have a thorough knowledge of the human heart, and make it speak properly; he should be a complete poet, without allowing any character in the play to sound like a poet; he should be a perfect master of his language, speak it with all its purity and with the utmost harmony, and yet he should not make the sense a slave to the rhyme. "Whoever," he added, "neglects any of these rules, though he may write two or three tragedies with tolerable success, will never be considered among the number of good authors. There are very few good tragedies; some are idylliums, in well written and harmonious dialogue; and others a chain of political reasonings that put one to sleep; or else pompous and high-flown amplifications that disgust rather than please. Still others are the ravings of a madman, barbarous in style, incoherent in meaning, or full of long speeches to the gods because the author doesn't know how to address mankind; in a word, a collection of false maxims and dull commonplace."

Candide listened to this discourse with great attention, and formed a high opinion of the person who delivered it; and as the Marchioness had taken care to place him near her side, he took the liberty to whisper to her softly in the ear, and ask who this person was who spoke so well. "He is a man of letters," replied her ladyship, "who never plays, and whom the Abbé brings to my house sometimes to spend an evening. He is a great judge of writing, especially in tragedy: he has written one himself, which was panned, and has written a book that was never seen out of his bookseller's shop, except for one copy, which was dedicated to me." "Oh, the great man!" cried Candide: "he is a second Pangloss."

Then turning towards him: "Sir," said he, "you are no doubt of the opinion that everything is for the best in the physical and moral world, and that nothing could be otherwise than it is?" "I, sir!" replied the man of letters; "think no such thing, I assure you; I find that everything goes wrong in our world. No one knows his place in society, his duty, nor what he does, nor what he should do; and except for our evenings, which are cheerful enough, the rest of our time is spent in idle disputes and quarrels: Jansenists against Molinists,[23] the Parliament against the Church, and one armed body of men against another; courtier against courtier, husband against wife, and relations against relations. In short, this world is nothing but one continuous scene of civil war."

"Yes," said Candide, "and I have seen worse than all that; and yet a learned man, who had the misfortune to be hanged, taught me that everything was marvellously well, and that these evils you are speaking of were only just the shadows in a beautiful picture." "Your hanged sage," said Martin, "laughed at you. These shadows, as you call them, are the most horrible blemishes." "It is men who make these blemishes," said Candide, "and they cannot do otherwise." "Then it is not their fault," added Martin. Most of the card players, who did not understand a syllable of this discourse, amused themselves with drinking, while Martin reasoned with the learned gentleman; and Candide entertained the lady of the house with a part of his adventures.

After supper the Marchioness conducted Candide into her dressing-room, and made him sit down under a canopy. "Well," she said, "are you still so madly in love with Miss Cunégonde of Thunder-ten-tronckh?" "Yes, madam," replied Candide. The Marchioness said to him, with a tender smile, "You answer me like a young man born in Westphalia. A Frenchman would have said, 'It is true, madam, I had been in love with Miss Cunégonde; but since I have seen you I fear I can no longer love her as I did.' " "Alas! madam," replied Candide, "I will answer in any way you want." "You fell in love with her, I find, in stooping to pick up her handkerchief, which she had dropped. You shall pick up my garter." "Gladly, madam," said Candide; and he picked it up. "But you must

tie it on again," said the lady. "Look, young man," said the Marchioness, "you are a stranger. I make some of my lovers here in
Paris languish for me for two weeks; but I surrender to you the first
night, because I am willing to do the honours of my country to a
young Westphalian." The fair one having cast her eye on two very
large diamonds that were on the young stranger's finger, praised
them in so earnest a manner that they were in an instant transferred
from his finger to hers.

As Candide was going home with the Abbé he felt some remorse
at having been unfaithful to Miss Cunégonde. The Abbé sympathized
with him in his uneasiness. He had only a small share of the fifty
thousand francs which Candide had lost at cards, and the two diamonds which had been in a manner extorted from him; and
therefore very cunningly schemed to make the most that he could
of his new acquaintance. He talked at length of Miss Cunégonde;
and Candide assured him that he would beg forgiveness for his
infidelity of that fair one when he saw her at Venice.

The Abbé overflowed with politeness, and seemed to interest
himself warmly in everything that Candide said, did, or seemed
inclined to do.

"And so, sir, you have an engagement at Venice?" "Yes, Mon-
sieur l'Abbé," answered Candide, "I must absolutely wait for Miss
Cunégonde;" and then, carried away by the pleasure he took in
talking about the object of his love, he recounted, as he often did,
part of his adventures with that illustrious Westphalian beauty.

"I suppose," said the Abbé, "Miss Cunégonde has a great deal of
wit, and that her letters must be very entertaining." "I never received any from her," said Candide, "for as you can imagine, being
expelled from the castle on her account, I could not write to her
especially because soon after my departure I heard that she was
dead; but, thank God, I found out afterwards that she was living. I
left her again after this, and now I have sent a messenger to her
nearly two thousand leagues from here, and I am waiting here for
his return with an answer from her."

The artful Abbé did not let a word of all this escape him, though
he seemed to be musing upon something else. He soon took his
leave of the two adventurers, after having embraced them with the

greatest cordiality. The next morning, almost as soon as his eyes were open, Candide received the following letter:—

"My dearest Lover,—I have been ill in this city for eight days. I have heard of your arrival, and would fly to your arms if were I able to move. I was told that you passed through Bordeaux on your way here; that was where I left the faithful Cacambo and the old woman, who will soon follow me. The Governor of Buenos Ayres has taken everything from me but your heart, which I still retain. Come to me immediately. Your presence will either give me new life or cause me to die of joy."

This unexpected letter filled Candide with utmost joy; though on the other hand, the illness of his beloved Miss Cunégonde overwhelmed him with grief. Torn between these two feelings, he took his gold and his diamonds, and hired a person to conduct him and Martin to the house where Miss Cénogunde lodged. Upon entering the room he felt his limbs tremble, his heart flutter, his tongue falter. He attempted to open the curtain, and asked for some light. "Lord, sir," cried a maid-servant, who was waiting in the room, "be careful; light will be the death of her." And so saying, she pulled the curtains closed again. "Cunégonde! my dear Cunégonde!" cried Candide, bathed in tears, "how are you? If you can't see me, at least speak to me." "Alas! she cannot speak," said the maid. The sick lady then put a plump hand out of the bed, and Candide first bathed it with his tears, then filled it with diamonds, leaving a purse of gold upon the chair.

In the midst of this emotional moment an officer came into the room, followed by the Abbé and a squad of musketeers. "There," he said, "are the two suspected foreigners." At the same time he ordered them to be seized and carried to prison. "Travellers are not treated in this manner in the country of El Dorado," said Candide. "I am more of a Manichæan now than ever," said Martin. "But, good sir, where are you taking us," said Candide. "To a dungeon, my dear sir," replied the officer.

When Martin had recovered a little, so that he was able to form a cool judgment of what had happened, he realized that the person who had acted the part of Miss Cunégonde was a cheat, that the Abbé of Perigord was another cheat, who had imposed on the

honest simplicity of Candide, and that the officer was still another
cheat, whom they might easily get rid of.

Candide, following the advice of his friend Martin, and burning
with impatience to see the real Miss Cunégonde, rather than have
to appear at a court of justice, offered the officer three small diamonds, each of them worth three thousand pistoles. "Ah, sir," said
this man, "even if you had committed every crime imaginable, this
would render you the most honest man in my eyes. Three diamonds
worth three thousand pistoles! Why, my dear sir, rather than take
you to jail, I would die for you. All foreigners get arrested here,
but let me manage things. I have a brother at Dieppe, in Normandy.
I myself will take you there, and if you have a diamond left to give
him, he will take care of you as I myself would."

"But why," said Candide, "do they arrest all foreigners?" The
Abbé of Perigord spoke up and said that it was because a beggar
from Atrebata* heard somebody tell foolish stories, and this induced
him to commit a parricide; not like the one in the month of May,
1610, but like the one in the month of December in 1594,[24] and
much on the order of several that had been committed in other
months and years by other poor devils who had heard foolish stories.

The officer then explained to them what that was all about. "Horrid monsters!" exclaimed Candide. "Is it possible that such scenes
could happen among a people who are perpetually singing and
dancing ? Can I flee this abominable country immediately, this execrable kingdom, where monkeys provoke tigers? I have seen bears
in my country, but men I have seen nowhere but in El Dorado. In
the name of God, sir," said he to the officer, "get me to Venice,
where I must wait for Miss Cunégonde." "Really, sir," replied the
officer, "I cannot possibly take you farther than Lower Normandy."
So saying, he ordered Candide's irons to be struck off, acknowledged himself mistaken, and dismissed his squad of followers; after
this he took Candide and Martin to Dieppe, and left them in the
care of his brother. There happened just then to be a small Dutch

---

*Latin name for the French province of Artois; Robert-François Damiens, who in
1757 failed in his attempt to assassinate Louis XV, came from Artois.

THE ARREST OF CANDIDE.

ship at anchor. The Norman, whom the other three diamonds had converted into the most helpful of men, made sure that Candide and his attendants got safely on board this vessel, which was just ready to sail for Portsmouth in England. This was not the nearest way to Venice indeed; but Candide felt that he'd just escaped from hell, and did not doubt that he would quickly find an opportunity to resume his voyage to Venice.

XXIII

Candide and Martin touch upon the English Coast; what they see there

"Ah, Pangloss! Pangloss! Ah, Martin! Martin! Ah, my dear Miss Cunégonde! What sort of a world is this?" exclaimed Candide as soon as he had boarded the Dutch ship. "Something very foolish and very abominable," said Martin. "You are acquainted with England," said Candide; "are they as great fools in that country as in France?" "Yes; but in a different way," answered Martin. "You know that these two nations are at war about a few acres of barren land near Canada, and that they have spent much more on that struggle than Canada is worth.[25] To say exactly if there are more people in one country or the other who should be in a madhouse exceeds the limits of my reasoning abilities. I know in general that the people we are going to visit are of a very dark and gloomy disposition."

As they were chatting thus together they arrived at Portsmouth. The shore on each side the harbour was lined with a multitude of people, whose eyes were steadfastly fixed on a big man who was kneeling down on the deck of one of the men-of-war with something tied over his eyes. In front of this man stood four soldiers, each of whom shot three bullets into his skull with full composure; and when it was done the crowds went away perfectly well satisfied.[26] "What is all this about?" said Candide; "and what demon is everywhere at work?" He then asked who was that big man who had just been killed with so much ceremony, when he received for answer that it was an admiral. "And why do you put your admiral to death?" "Because he did not put a sufficient number of people to death. You must know, he battled against French admiral, and it has been proved that he was not near enough to his antagonist." "But," replied Candide, "the French admiral must have been as far from the English admiral as the English admiral was from the French." "There is no doubt about that; but in this country it is necessary, now and then, to put one admiral to death in order to inspire the others to fight."

Candide was so shocked at what he saw and heard that he would not set foot on shore, but made a bargain with the Dutch skipper (without even caring if he robbed him like the captain of Surinam) to take him directly to Venice.

The skipper was ready in two days. They sailed along the coast of France, and passed within sight of Lisbon, at which Candide trembled. From there they proceeded to the straits, entered the Mediterranean, and at length they arrived at Venice. "God be praised," said Candide, embracing Martin, "this is the place where I am to see my beloved Cunégonde once again. I trust Cacambo as I do myself. All is well—all very well; all as well as possible."

XXIV

About Pacquette and Friar Giroflée

Upon their arrival in Venice he went in search of Cacambo at every inn and coffee-house, and among all the ladies of pleasure; but he found no trace of him. Every day he inquired about what ships had come in; still no news of Cacambo. "It is strange," he said to Martin, "very strange that I have had time to sail from Surinam to Bordeaux; to travel from there to Paris, to Dieppe, to Portsmouth; to sail along the coast of Portugal and Spain, and up the Mediterranean to spend a few months in Venice; and that my lovely Cunégonde has not yet arrived. Instead of her, I have only met with a Parisian impostor and a rascally Abbé of Perigord. Cunégonde is actually dead, and nothing remains for me too but death. Alas! how much better it would have been for me to have remained in the paradise of El Dorado, than to have returned to this wicked Europe! You are right, my dear Martin; you are certainly in the right: all is misery and deceit."

He fell into a deep melancholy, and neither went to the fashionable operas, nor took part in any of the diversions of the Carnival: not a single woman tempted him in the least bit. Martin said to him, "I think you are very foolish to imagine that a rascally valet, with five or six millions in his pocket, would go in search of your mistress to the far end of the world, and bring her to Venice to meet you. If he finds her, he will take her for himself; if he does not, he will take another. Let me advise you to forget your valet Cacambo, and your mistress Cunégonde." Martin's speech was not the most consolatory to the dejected Candide. His melancholy increased, and Martin never tired of showing him, that there is very little virtue or happiness in this world—except, perhaps in El Dorado, where hardly anybody can go.

While they were disputing on this important subject, and still expecting Miss Cunégonde, Candide noticed a young Theatin* friar in St. Mark's place, with a girl under his arm. The Theatin looked fresh-colored, plump and vigorous; his eyes sparkled; his air and gait were bold and lofty. The girl was very pretty, and was singing a song; and every now and then gave her Theatin an amorous ogle, and wantonly pinched his ruddy cheeks. "You will at least admit," said Candide to Martin, "that these two are happy. So far I have met with none but unfortunate people in the whole habitable globe, except in El Dorado; but as to this couple, I would venture to lay a wager that they are happy." "I bet they are not!" said Martin. "Well, we just have to ask them to dine with us," said Candide, "and you will see whether I am mistaken or not."

He approached them, and with great politeness invited them to his inn to eat some macaroni, with Lombard partridges and caviare, and to drink a bottle of Montepulciano, Lacryma Christi, Cyprus and Samos wine. The girl blushed; the Theatin accepted the invitation, and she followed him, eyeing Candide every now and then with a mixture of surprise and confusion, while the tears stole down her cheeks. No sooner did she enter his apartment than she cried out: "Mr. Candide, have you quite forgotten your Pacquette? Do you not recognize her again?" Candide, who had not looked carefully at her before, being wholly preoccupied with the thoughts of his dear Cunégonde. "Ah! is it you, child? Was it you that reduced Doctor Pangloss to that fine condition I saw him in?"

"Alas, sir," answered Pacquette, "it was indeed. I see that you already know everything; and I have been informed of all the misfortunes that happened to the whole family of my lady baroness and the fair Cunégonde. But I can safely swear to you that my fate was no less unhappy; I was innocence itself when you saw me last. A Cordelier, who was my confessor, easily misled me; the consequences proved terrible. I was obliged to leave the castle some time after the baron kicked you out of there; and if a famous surgeon had not taken pity on me, I would have been a dead woman. Gratitude obliged me to live with him some time as a companion. His wife, who was jealous to a point of rage, beat me mercilessly every

---

*The Theatins were a Catholic order founded in 1524 to combat the Protestant Reformation.

day. Oh! she was a perfect fury. The doctor himself was the ugliest of all mortals, and I the most wretched creature existing, to be continually beaten for a man I did not love. You know, sir, how dangerous it was for an ill-natured woman to be married to a physician. Incensed at the behaviour of his wife, one day he gave her so potent a remedy for a slight cold she had caught that she died in less than two hours in most dreadful convulsions. Her relations prosecuted the husband, who had to flee, and I was sent to prison. My innocence would not have saved me, if I had not been rather attractive. The judge set me free on condition that he should become the doctor's successor. However, I was soon replaced by a rival, dismissed without a farthing, and obliged to continue the abominable trade which you men think so pleasing, but which to us unhappy creatures is the most dreadful of all sufferings. Finally I came to work this business in Venice. Ah! sir! if you could know what it is like to be with every man—with old tradesmen, with counsellors, with monks, watermen, and abbés; to be exposed to all their insolence and abuse; to be reduced to borrowing a skirt only in order for it to be lifted by some disgusting man; to be robbed by one man of what was gained from another; to be subject to the extortions of civil magistrates; and to have for ever before one's eyes the prospect of old age, a hospital, or a dunghill, you would conclude that I am one of the most unhappy wretches breathing."

Thus Pacquette unburdened herself to honest Candide in his room, in the presence of Martin, who took occasion to say to him, "You see, I have won the wager already."

Friar Giroflée was all this time in the parlour refreshing himself with a glass or two of wine till dinner was ready. "But," said Candide to Pacquette, "you looked so happy and content when I met you, you sang and caressed the Theatin with so much fondness, that I absolutely thought you as happy as you say you are now miserable." "Ah, dear sir," said Pacquette, "this is one of the miseries of the trade; yesterday I was stripped and beaten by an officer, yet today I must appear in good humor in order to please a friar."

Candide was convinced, and acknowledged that Martin was right. They sat down to dinner with Pacquette and the Theatin; the meal was very agreeable, and towards the end they began to speak freely

among themselves. "Father," said Candide to the friar, "you seem
to me to enjoy a state of happiness that even kings might envy; joy
and health are painted on your countenance. You have a beautiful
friend to divert you; and you seem to be perfectly well contented
with your condition as a Theatin."

"Faith, sir," said Friar Giroflée, "I wish with all my soul that all
the Theatins were at the bottom of the sea. I have been tempted a
thousand times to set fire to the convent and go and turn Turk. My
parents forced me at the age of fifteen to put on this detestable robe,
only to increase the fortune of an elder brother of mine, may God
confound him! Jealousy, discord and fury reside in our convent. It
is true I have often preached paltry sermons which earned me a
little money, part of which the prior robs me of, and the remainder
helps to buy my joys; but at night when I go to my convent, I am
ready to dash my brains against the walls of the dormitory; and this
is the case with all the rest of our fraternity."

Martin, turning towards Candide with his usual coolness, said,
"Well, what think you now? Have I won the wager entirely?" Candide gave two thousand piastres to Pacquette and a thousand to Friar
Giroflée, saying, "I will answer that this will make them happy." "I
don't believe so," said Martin; "perhaps this money will only make
them wretched." "Be that as it may," said Candide, "one thing
comforts me; I see that one often meets with those whom we never
expected to see again; so that perhaps, as I have found my red sheep
and Pacquette, I may be lucky enough to find Miss Cunégonde also."
"I hope," said Martin, "that one day she will make you happy, but
I doubt it very much." "You are very hard in your beliefs," said
Candide. "It is because," said Martin, "I have seen the world."

"Observe those gondoliers," said Candide; "aren't they always
singing?" "You do not see them," answered Martin, "at home with
their wives and brats. The doge* has his chagrin, gondoliers theirs.
Nevertheless, in general I look upon the gondolier's life as preferable
to that of the doge; but the difference is so trifling that it is not
worth the trouble of looking into it."

"I have heard a lot," said Candide "of the Senator Pococuranté,†

---

*Chief magistrate of Venice.
†Based on Italian words; signifies "who could not care less."

who lives in that fine house at the Brenta, where they say he entertains foreigners in the most polite manner. They claim this man has never known a moment of sorrow." "I would like to see so extraordinary a being," said Martin. Candide promptly sent a messenger to Signor Pococuranté, asking permission to see him the next day.

XXV

Candide and Martin pay a visit to Signor Pococuranté, a noble Venetian

Candide and his friend Martin went into a gondola on the Brenta, and arrived at the palace of the noble Pococuranté: the gardens were laid out in elegant taste, and adorned with fine marble statues; his palace was one of beautiful architecture. The master of the house, who was a man of sixty, and very rich, received our two travellers with great politeness, but without much eagerness, which somewhat disconcerted Candide, but was not at all displeasing to Martin.

As soon as they were seated, two very pretty girls, neatly dressed, brought in chocolate, which was extremely well frothed. Candide could not help praising their beauty and grace. "They are pretty good creatures," said the senator. "I make them my companions, for I am tired of the ladies of the town, their coquetry, their jealousy, their quarrels, their humours, their meannesses, their pride, and their folly. I am weary of making sonnets, or of paying for sonnets to be made on them; but after all, these two girls are beginning to bore me."

After lunch, Candide walked through a large gallery, where he was amazed by the beauty of the paintings. Candide asked who the painter of the two finest was. "They are Raphael's,"* answered the senator. "I spent a great deal of money on them seven years ago, purely out of curiosity as they were said to be the finest pieces in Italy; but I cannot say they please me; the colouring is dark and heavy; the figures do not swell or come out enough; and the drapery is very bad. In short, regardless of the praises lavished upon them, they are not, in my opinion, a true representation of nature. I ap-

---

*Raphael Sanzio (1483–1529), one of the greatest painters of the Italian Renaissance.

prove of no paintings except those where I think I see Nature herself; and there are very few, if any, of that kind. I have what is
called a fine collection, but I take no manner of delight in them."

While dinner was getting ready Pococuranté ordered a concerto
to be performed. Candide found the music delightful. "This noise,"
said the noble Venetian, "may amuse one for a little while, but if
it was to last more than half-an-hour, it would grow tiresome to
everybody, though perhaps no one would care to admit that. Music
has become only the art of performing what is difficult; and whatever is difficult cannot please for long.

"I believe I might take more pleasure in an opera, if they had
not found ways to make it monstrous and revolting to me; and I
am amazed at how people can bear to see bad tragedies set to music;
where the scenes are contrived for no other reason than to introduce
three or four ridiculous songs, to give a favourite actress an opportunity of showing off her voice. Let who will or can swoon with
pleasure at the trills of a eunuch quavering through the majestic part
of Cæsar* or Cato,† and strutting in a foolish manner upon the stage.
For my part, I have long ago renounced these paltry entertainments,
which constitute the glory of modern Italy, and are so dearly purchased by crowned heads." Candide disputed these sentiments; but
he did it in a discreet manner. As for Martin, he was entirely of the
old senator's opinion.

Dinner being served, they sat down to the table, and after a hearty
meal, returned to the library. Candide, seeing a copy of Homer‡ in
splendid binding, complimented the noble Venetian's taste. "This,"
said he, "is a book that was once the delight of the great Pangloss,
the best philosopher in Germany." "Homer is no favourite of
mine," answered Pococuranté very coolly. "I was made to believe
once that I took a pleasure in reading him; but his continual repe-
titions of battles which are all alike; his gods that are always inter-

---

*Julius Caesar (100–44 B.C.), Roman statesman and general.
†Cato the Younger, also known as Cato of Utica (95–46 B.C.), Roman statesman
and enemy of Julius Caesar.
‡Great figure of ancient Greek literature and presumed author of the *Iliad* and the
Odyssey, epic poems ranked among the supreme literary achievements of Western
literature.

fering, but never doing anything decisive; his Helen, who is the cause of the war, and yet hardly acts in the whole performance; his Troy that holds out so long without being taken; in short, all these things together make the poem very boring to me. I have asked some scholars if reading it bored them as much as it bored me. Those who spoke sincerely assured me that he had made them fall asleep, and yet that they could not well avoid giving him a place in their libraries; but that is merely what they do with an antique, like those rusty medals which are kept only for curiosity, and are of no use in commerce."

"But your excellency does not hold the same opinion of Virgil?" said Candide. "I concede," replied Pococuranté, "that the second, third, fourth, and sixth books of his Aeneid are excellent; but as for his pious Aeneas, his strong Cloanthus, his friendly Achates, his boy Ascanius, his silly king Latinus, his ill-bred Amata, his insipid Lavinia, and some other characters much in the same strain, I don't believe there was ever anything more flat and disagreeable. I must confess I prefer Tasso and even that sleepy tale-teller Ariosto."[27]

"May I take the liberty to ask if you do not get great pleasure from reading Horace?" said Candide. "There are maxims there," replied Pococuranté, "from which a man of the world may reap some benefit; and the short measure of the verse makes them more easily remembered. But I see nothing extraordinary in his journey to Brundusium, and his description of his bad dinner; nor in his dirty low quarrel between one Rupilius, whose words, as he expresses it, were full of poisonous filth; and another, whose language was dipped in vinegar. His indelicate verses against old women and witches have frequently given me great offence;[28] nor can I see what's so great about his telling his friend Maecenas* that, if he is raised by him to the ranks of lyric poets, his lofty head shall touch the stars.† Fods admire everything in an esteemed writer. I read only to please myself. I like only what suits me." Candide, who had been raised never to judge for himself, was astonished at what he heard;

---

*Wealthy Roman (c.70–8 B.C.); friend and patron of Virgil and Horace.
†Reference to Horace's *Odes* (book 1, ode 1, lines 35–36): *Sublimi feriam sidera vertice*, Latin for "I shall strike the stars with my forehead."

but Martin found that there was a good deal of reason in the senator's remarks.

"Oh, here is a copy of Cicero!*" said Candide; "this great man, I assume, you are never tired of reading." "Indeed, I never read him at all," replied Pococuranté. "What do I care whether he pleads for Rabirius or Cluentius? As a judge, I have enough trials. I might like his philosophical works better; but when I realized that he had doubts about everything, I figured I knew as much as himself, and had no need of a guide to learn ignorance."

"Ha!" cried Martin, "here are eighty volumes of the Memoirs of the Academy of Sciences; perhaps there may be something curious and valuable in this collection." "Yes," answered Pococuranté, "so there might, if any one of the authors of this rubbish had only invented the art of pin-making. But all these volumes are filled with empty systems, without one single useful thing."

"I see a lot of plays," said Candide, "in Italian, Spanish and French." "Yes," replied the Venetian; "there are I think three thousand, and not three dozen of them good for anything. As to those huge volumes of divinity, and those enormous collections of sermons, altogether they are not worth one single page of Seneca;† and I'm sure you will readily believe that neither myself nor anyone else ever opens them."

Martin, seeing some shelves filled with English books, said to the senator: "I suppose that a republican must be delighted with the majority of those books written in a land of liberty." "It is noble to write as we think," said Pococuranté; "it is the privilege of humanity. Throughout Italy we write only what we do not think; and the present inhabitants of the country of the Cæsars and Antoninuses‡ dare not acquire a single idea without the permission of a Father Dominican.§ I would be enamoured of the freedom inspired

---

*Marcus Tullius Cicero, Roman senator and orator (106–43 B.C.).
†Lucius Annaeus Seneca (c.4 B.C.–A.D. 65), Roman philosopher, dramatist, and statesman.
‡References to two Roman statesmen and soldiers: Julius Caesar (100–44 B.C.) and Marc Antony (c.82–30 B.C.).
§The Order of the Dominicans was instrumental in organizing the Inquisition.

by English genius if passion and partisan spirit did not corrupt all that is estimable in this precious liberty."

Candide, seeing an edition of a Milton,* asked the senator if he did not consider that author a great man. "Who?" said Pococuranté sharply. "That barbarian, who writes a tedious commentary, in ten books of rambling verse, on the first chapter of Genesis! That slovenly imitator of the Greeks, who disfigures creation by making the Messiah take a pair of compasses from Heaven's cupboard in order to plan the world while Moses represents the Deity as creating the world with a word! You expect me to admire a writer who has spoiled Tasso's hell and devil; who transforms Lucifer, sometimes into a toad, and at other times into a pigmy; who makes him say the same thing a hundred times over; who makes him argue theology: and who, by an absurdly serious imitation of Ariosto's comic invention of fire-arms, has the devils firing cannon in heaven! Neither I, nor any other Italian, can possibly take pleasure in such melancholy reveries. But the marriage of sin and death, and snakes that sin gives birth to, are enough to make any person sick whose taste is at all refined. This obscene, whimsical, and disagreeable poem met with the disdain that it deserved at its first publication; and I only treat the author now as he was treated in his own country by his contemporaries."

Candide was grieved at this speech, as he had a great respect for Homer and was very fond of Milton. "Alas!" said he very softly to Martin, "I am afraid this man holds our German poets in great contempt." "There would be no great harm in that," said Martin. "Oh, what a surprising man!" said Candide to himself; "what a great genius this Pococuranté must be! Nothing can please him."

After finishing their survey of the library, they went down into the garden, and Candide praised its beauties. "I know nothing on earth laid out in such bad taste," said Pococuranté, "everything about it is childish and trifling; but I will have another laid out tomorrow on a nobler plan."

As soon as our travellers had taken leave of his excellency,

---

*John Milton (1608–1674), one of the great English poets. The paragraph refers to Milton's *Paradise Lost*; the epic poem appeared in ten books in 1667 and was expanded to twelve in 1674.

"Well," said Candide to Martin, "I hope you will own that this man is the happiest of all mortals, for he is above everything he possesses." "But don't you see," answered Martin, "that he dislikes everything he possesses? Plato said a long time ago that the best stomachs are not those which refuse all food." "True," said Candide, "but still there must certainly be a pleasure in criticising everything, and in seeing faults where others think they see beauties." "That is," replied Martin, "there is a pleasure in having no pleasure." "Well, well," said Candide, "I find that I will be the only happy man at last, when I am blessed with the sight of my dear Cunégonde." "It is good to hope," said Martin.

In the meantime, days and weeks passed away, and no news of Cacambo. Candide was so overwhelmed with grief that he did not notice that Pacquette and Friar Giroflée had never returned and thanked him.

XXVI

Candide and Martin sup with six strangers; and who they were

One evening when Candide and Martin were going to sit down to supper with some foreigners who lodged at the same inn where they were staying, a man, with a face the colour of soot, came behind him, and taking him by the arm, said "Be ready to leave with us; don't miss this." He turned around and saw Cacambo. Nothing but the sight of Miss Cunégonde could have given him greater joy and surprise. He was almost beside himself. After embracing this dear friend, "Cunégonde!" he said, "Cunégonde has come with you, no doubt! Where, where is she? Take me to her this instant so that I may die of joy in her presence." "Cunégonde is not here," answered Cacambo, "she is at Constantinople." "Good heavens, at Constantinople! But no matter if she were in China, I would fly there. Quick, quick, dear Cacambo, let's go." "We will leave after eating," said Cacambo. "I cannot at present say anything more to you. I am a slave, and my master waits for me: I must go and wait on him at table. But mum! say not a word; only get your supper, and be ready."

Candide, divided between joy and grief, charmed to have thus met his faithful agent again, and surprised to hear he was a slave, his heart palpitating, his senses confused, but full of the hopes of recovering his dear Cunégonde, sat down to eat with Martin, who watched all these scenes cooly, and with six strangers, who had come to spend the Carnival at Venice.

Cacambo, who was pouring a drink for one of these strangers, drew near to his master when the meal was nearly over, and whispered to him in the ear, "Sire, your majesty may go when you please; the ship is ready"; and so saying, he left the room. The guests, surprised at what they had heard, looked at each other without speaking a word, when another servant drawing near to his master, in like manner said, "Sire, your majesty's post-chaise is at Padua, and the bark is ready." The master made a sign and the servant instantly withdrew. The diners all stared at each other again, and the general astonishment was increased. A third servant then approached another of the strangers, and said, "Sire, believe me, your Majesty should not stay here any longer; I will go and get everything ready," and instantly disappeared.

Candide and Martin had no doubt now that this was some of the diversions of the Carnival, and that these were characters in masquerade. Then a fourth domestic said to the fourth stranger, "Your majesty may set off when you please"; saying this, he went away like the rest. A fifth valet said the same to a fifth master. But the sixth domestic spoke in a different style to the person on whom he waited, and who sat near to Candide. "My word, sir," said he, "they will give no more credit to your majesty or to me, and we could both wind up in jail this very night; and therefore I've got to take care of myself, and so adieu." With the servants all gone, the six strangers, with Candide and Martin, remained in a profound silence. Finally Candide broke it by saying, "Gentlemen, this is a very singular joke, upon my word; why, how came you all to be kings? For my part I assure you that neither my friend Martin here nor myself have any claim to royalty."

Cacambo's master then began, with great gravity, to speak in Italian: "I am not joking in the least. My name is Achmet III.* I was grand seignor for many years; I dethroned my brother, my nephew dethroned me, my viziers lost their heads, and I am condemned to end my days in the old seraglio. My nephew, the Grand Sultan Mahomet, gives me permission to travel sometimes for my health, and I am here to spend the Carnival at Venice."

A young man who sat by Achmet spoke next, and said: "My name is Ivan.† I was once Emperor of all the Russias, but was dethroned while still in my cradle. My parents were locked up, and I was brought up in a prison; yet I am sometimes allowed to travel,

---

*Ottoman sultan (1673–1736), deposed in 1730. "Viziers" were ministers of state in Muslim countries.

†Ivan VI (1740–1764); as an infant, proclaimed czar; deposed in 1741, after which he was imprisoned for the rest of his life; executed in 1764.

though always with persons to keep a guard over me, and I am here to spend the Carnival at Venice."

The third said: "I am Charles-Edward, King of England;* my father ceded his royal rights to me. I have fought in defence of my rights, and near a thousand of my friends have had their hearts taken out of their bodies alive, and thrown into their faces. I have myself been confined in a prison. I am going to Rome to visit the king my father, who was dethroned as well as myself and my grandfather; and I am here to spend the Carnival at Venice."

The fourth spoke thus: "I am the King of Poland;[†] the fortune of war has stripped me of my hereditary dominions. My father experienced the same vicissitudes of fate. I resign myself to the will of Providence, in the same manner as Sultan Achmet, the Emperor Ivan, and King Charles Edward, to whom, I hope, God gives long lives; and I am here to spend the Carnival at Venice."

The fifth said: "I am King of Poland also.[‡] I have twice lost my kingdom; but Providence has given me other dominions, where I have done more good than all the Sarmatian kings put together ever managed to do on the banks of the Vistula. I resign myself likewise to Providence; and am here to spend the Carnival at Venice."

It now came to the sixth monarch's turn to speak. "Gentlemen," said he, "I am not so great a prince as the rest of you, it is true, but I am, however, a crowned head. I am Theodore, elected king of Corsica.[§] I have had the title of majesty, and am now barely treated with common civility. I have coined money and am not now worth a single ducat. I have had two secretaries, and am now without a valet. I was once seated on a throne, and since then have lain upon a truss of straw in a common jail in London, and I very much

---

*Reference to Charles-Edward-Stuart (1720–1788), known as Bonnie Prince Charlie and the Young Pretender.

[†]Reference to Augustus III (1696–1763), elector of Saxony and king of Poland; lost Saxony; dethroned by Frederick the Great in 1756.

[‡]Reference to Stanislaw I Leszczynski (1677–1766), father-in-law of Louis XV, driven off the throne of Poland in 1736 and subsequently made duke of Lorraine.

[§]Baron Theodor von Neuhof (1694–1756), Westphalian adventurer elected king of Corsica in 1736; ruled for about eight months; tried unsuccessfully to regain the throne; lived in poverty in England after 1749.

fear I shall meet with the same fate here in Venice, where I've come, like your majesties, to divert myself at the Carnival."

The other five kings listened to this speech with great attention; it excited their compassion; each of them made the unhappy Theodore a present of twenty sequins, and Candide gave him a diamond worth just a hundred times that sum. "Who can this private person be?" said the five princes to one another, "who is able to give, and has actually given, an hundred times as much as any of us?"

Just as they rose from the table, in came four serene highnesses, who had also been stripped of their territories by the fortunes of war, and who had come to spend the remainder of the Carnival at Venice. Candide took no manner of notice of them; he was concerned only with his voyage to Constantinople, where he intended to go in search of his lovely Miss Cunégonde.

XXVII

Candide's Voyage to Constantinople

The trusty Cacambo had already made arrangements with the captain of the Turkish ship that was to carry Sultan Achmet back to Constantinople, to take Candide and Martin on board. Accordingly, they both boarded ship, after paying their respects to his miserable highness. As they were going on board, Candide said to Martin: "You see we ate in company with six dethroned kings, and to one of them I gave charity. Perhaps there may be a great many other princes still more unfortunate. For my part, I have lost only a hundred sheep, and am now going to fly to the arms of my charming Miss Cunégonde. My dear Martin, I must insist on it that Pangloss was right. All is for the best." "I hope so," said Martin. "But this was an odd adventure that we met with in Venice. I do not think there has ever before been an instance of six dethroned monarchs eating together at a public inn." "This is not more extraordinary," said Martin, "than most of what has happened to us. It is a very common thing for kings to be dethroned; and as for our having the honour to eat with six of them, it is a mere accident which doesn't deserve our attention."

As soon as Candide set foot on board the vessel he flew to his old friend and valet, Cacambo; and throwing his arms around his neck, embraced him with joy. "Well," said he, "what news of Miss Cunégonde? Is she still the paragon of beauty? Does she love me still? How is she? You have no doubt purchased a superb palace for her at Constantinople?"

"My dear master," replied Cacambo, "Miss Cunégonde washes dishes on the banks of the Propontis,* in the house of a prince who

---

*The Sea of Marmora, between the Bosphorus and the Dardanelles.

has very few to wash. She is at present a slave in the family of an ancient sovereign named Ragotsky,[29] whom the grand Turk allows three crowns a day to maintain him in his exile; but the most melancholy circumstance of all this is that she has turned horribly ugly." "Ugly or handsome," said Candide, "I am a man of honour; and, as such, am obliged to love her still. But how could she have possibly been reduced to so abject a condition when I sent five or six millions to her by you?" "Well," said Cacambo, "wasn't I obliged to give two millions to Seignor Don Fernando d'Ibaraa y Fagueora y Mascarenes y Lampourdos y Souza, the Governor of Buenos Ayres, for his permission to take Miss Cunégonde away with me? And then didn't a pirate very gallantly strip us of all the rest? And then didn't this same pirate carry us with him to Cape Matapan, to Milo, to Nicaria, to Samos, to Petra, to the Dardanelles, to Marmora, to Scutari? Miss Cunégonde and the old woman are now servants to the prince I have told you of, and I myself am slave to the dethroned Sultan." "What a chain of shocking accidents!" exclaimed Candide. "But, after all, I still have some diamonds left, with which I can easily buy Miss Cunégonde's liberty. It is a pity, though, she is grown so very ugly."

Then turning to Martin, he asked, "What do you think? Whose condition is most to be pitied, the Emperor Achmet's, the Emperor Ivan's, King Charles Edward's, or mine?" "I don't know at all," said Martin. "I would need to enter the heart of each man to know." "Ah!" cried Candide, "were Pangloss here now, he would have known and satisfied me at once." "I don't know," said Martin, "what scales your Pangloss would use to weigh the misfortunes of mankind, and set a value on their sufferings. All that I pretend to know of the matter is that there are millions of men on the earth whose conditions are a hundred times more pitiable than those of King Charles Edward, the Emperor Ivan, or Sultan Achmet." "You may very well be right," answered Candide.

In a few days they reached the Bosphorous. Candide began by re-purchasing Cacambo at a very high price; then, without losing time, he and his companions went on board a galley in order to search for his Cunégonde on the banks of the Propontis, however ugly she may have grown.

There were two slaves among the crew of the galley, who rowed very poorly, and to whose bare backs the master of the vessel frequently applied a few lashes with a bullwhip. Candide naturally looked at these two slaves more attentively than at any of the rest, and out of pity moved closer to them. Certain features of their disfigured faces appeared to him to bear a resemblance to those of Pangloss and the unhappy Baron Jesuit, Miss Cunégonde's brother. This notion moved and saddened him. He examined them more attentively than before. "In truth," said he to Cacambo, "if I had not seen my master Pangloss hanged, and had not myself been unlucky enough to kill the Baron, I should absolutely think that those two rowers were the men."

No sooner had Candide uttered the names of the Baron and Pangloss than the two slaves gave a great cry, ceased rowing, and dropped their oars from their hands. The master of the vessel seeing this, ran up to them, and redoubled the discipline of the bullwhip. "Stop, stop," cried Candide, "I will give you as much money as you want." "Good heavens! it is Candide," said one of the men. "Candide!" cried the other. "Do I dream?" said Candide, "or am I awake? Am I actually on board this galley? Is this my Lord Baron whom I killed? and that my Master Pangloss, whom I saw hanged?"

"It is I! it is I!" they both cried together. "What, is this your great philosopher?" said Martin. "Sir," said Candide to the captain of the ship, "how much do you want for the ransom of the Baron of Thunder-ten-tronckh, who is one of the first barons of the empire, and Mr. Pangloss, the most profound metaphysician in Germany?" "Why, then, Christian cur," replied the Turkish captain, "since these two dogs of Christian slaves are barons and metaphysicians, who are no doubt of high rank in their own country, you will give me fifty thousand sequins."

"You will have them, sir; take me back as quickly as possible to Constantinople, and you will receive the money immediately. Or, no! take me to Miss Cunégonde." The captain, at Candide's first word, had turned his ship around, and he made the crew ply their oars so quickly that the vessel flew through the water quicker than a bird cleaves the air.

Candide embraced the Baron and Pangloss a hundred times. "And so, then, my dear Baron, I did not kill you? And you, my dear Pangloss, how can you be alive after your hanging? And why are you slaves on board a Turkish galley?" "Is it true that my dear sister is in this country?" said the Baron. "Yes," said Cacambo. "And do I once again see my dear Candide?" said Pangloss. Candide presented Martin and Cacambo to them. They embraced each other, and all spoke together. The galley flew, and already they were back in port. Candide instantly sent for a Jew, and for fifty thousand sequins sold him a diamond worth one hundred thousand, though the buyer swore to him by Father Abraham that he gave him the most he could possibly afford. Candide immediately ransomed the Baron and Pangloss. The latter flung himself at the feet of his deliverer, and bathed him with his tears. The former thanked him with a gracious nod, and promised to return the money at the first opportunity. "But is it possible?" said he, "that my sister is in Turkey?" "Nothing is more possible," answered Cacambo, "since she is the dishwasher in the house of a Transylvanian prince." Candide sent for two Jews, and sold more diamonds to them. And then he set out with his companions in another galley, to free Miss Cunégonde from slavery.

XXVIII

What happened to Candide, Cunégonde, Pangloss, Martin, etc.

"Pardon me," said Candide to the Baron; "once more let me beg your pardon, reverend father, for having run you through the body with my sword." "Say no more about it," replied the Baron; "I was a little too hasty, I admit. But as you seem to want to know how I came to be a slave on board the galley where you saw me, I will tell you. After I had been cured of the wound you gave me by the college apothecary, I was attacked and carried off by a party of Spanish troops, who put me in prison in Buenos Ayres, at the very time my sister was leaving there. I asked permission to return to Rome, from the general of my order. He instead appointed me chaplain to the French ambassador at Constantinople. I had not been a week in my new office when I happened to meet one evening a young Icoglan,* who was extremely handsome and well made. The weather was very hot; the young man wanted to swim. I took the opportunity to swim with him. I did not know it was a crime for a Christian to be found naked with a young Turk. A cadi sentenced me to receive a hundred blows on the soles of my feet, and sent me to the galleys. I do not believe there was ever an act of more flagrant injustice. But I would like to know how my sister came to be a kitchen maid to a Transylvanian prince who had taken refuge among the Turks."

"But you, my dear Pangloss," said Candide. "How is it possible that I see you again?" "It is true," answered Pangloss, "you saw me hanged, though I should have been burnt; but you may remember

---

*Page of the Sultan.

that it rained extremely hard when they were going to roast me. The storm was so violent that they found it impossible to light the fire, so they hanged me because they could do no better. A surgeon purchased my body, carried it home, and prepared to dissect me. He began by making a crucial incision from my navel to the clavicle. It is impossible for any one to have been more lamely hanged than I had been. The executioner of the holy Inquisition was a sub-deacon, and knew how to burn people very well; but as for hanging, he was a novice; the rope was wet and not slipping properly, and the noose did not join. In short, I was still breathing; the crucial incision made me scream to such a degree that my surgeon fell flat upon his back; and imagining that it was the devil he was dissecting, he ran away, and in his fright tumbled downstairs. His wife, hearing the noise, ran in from the next room, and seeing me stretched upon the table with my crucial incision, was more terrified than her husband, fled and fell over him. When they had recovered a little, I heard her say to her husband, 'My dear, how could you think of dissecting a heretic? Don't you know that the devil is always in them? I'll go directly to get a priest to come and drive the evil spirit out.' I trembled from head to foot at hearing her talk in this manner, and I exerted what little strength I had left to cry out, 'Have mercy on me!' At length the Portuguese barber* took courage, sewed up my wound, and his wife nursed me: and I was back on my feet in two week's time. The barber got me a job as a lackey to a Knight of Malta,† who was going to Venice; but finding my master had no money to pay me my wages, I entered into the service of a Venetian merchant, and went with him to Constantinople.

"One day I happened to enter a mosque, where I saw no one but an old imam‡ and a very pretty young female worshipper, who was saying her prayers; her neck was quite bare, and between her two breasts she had a beautiful bouquet of tulips, roses, anemones, ranunculuses, hyacinths, and auriculas; she dropped her bouquet. I picked it up and presented it to her with the most respectful bow. I was so long in putting it back in place that the imam began to be

---

*Barber-surgeon; barbers were originally also surgeons.
†Religious and military order of Malta that originated with the Crusades.
‡Muslim priest.

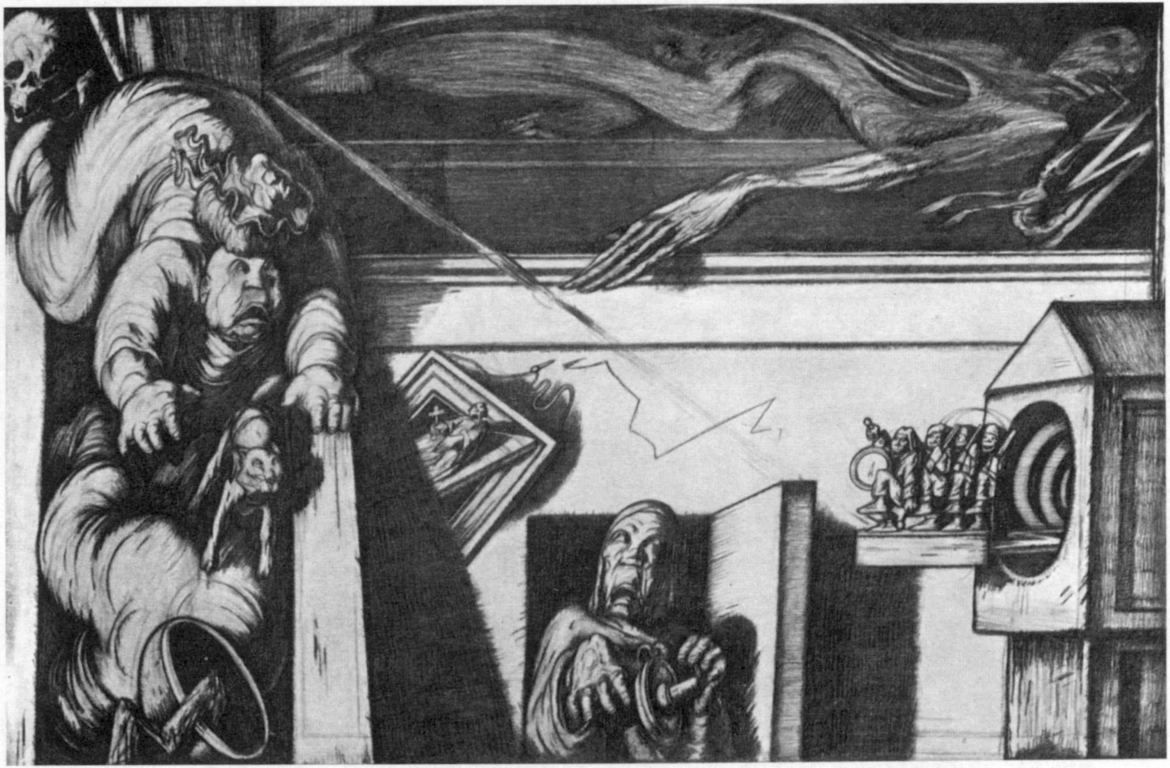

THE CRUCIAL INCISION

angry, and seeing that I was a Christian, he cried out for help; they carried me before the Cadi, who ordered me to receive one hundred blows on the soles of my feet and sent me to the galleys. I was chained in the very galley and to the very same bench with the Baron. On board this galley there were four young men from Marseilles, five Neapolitan priests, and two monks of Corfu, who told us that these kinds of adventures happened every day. The Baron claimed that he had suffered a greater injustice than I; and insisted that there was far less harm in picking up a bouquet and putting it into a young woman's bosom, than in being found stark naked with a young Icoglan. We were continually whipped, and received twenty lashes a day with a bullwhip, when the chain of events within this universe brought you on board our galley to ransom us from slavery."

"Well, my dear Pangloss," Candide said to them, "when you were hanged, dissected, whipped, and tugging at the oar, did you continue to think that everything in this world happens for the best?" "I have always abided by my first opinion," answered Pangloss; "for, after all, I am a philosopher, and it would not become me to retract my sentiments, especially since Leibniz could not be wrong, and besides pre-established harmony is the finest thing in the world, as well as a *plenum* and the *materia subtilis*."[30]

XXIX

In what manner Candide found Miss Cunégonde
and the Old Woman again

While Candide, the Baron, Pangloss, Martin, and Cacambo were relating their adventures, and reasoning on the contingent or non-contingent events of this world,[31] on causes and effects, on moral and physical evil, on free-will and necessity, and on the consolation available to a slave on a Turkish galley, they arrived at the house of the Transylvanian prince on the coasts of the Propontis. The first objects they saw there were Miss Cunégonde and the old woman, who were hanging out some table-cloths on a line to dry.

The Baron turned pale at the sight. Even the tender Candide, that affectionate lover, upon seeing his fair Cunégonde all sun-burnt, with bloodshot eyes, a withered neck, her face wrinkled, and her arms red and scaly, started back with horror; but recovering himself, he advanced towards her out of good manners. She embraced Candide and her brother; they embraced the old woman, and Candide ransomed them both.

There was a small farm in the neighbourhood which the old woman suggested to Candide as accommodation till the company should meet with some better fate. Cunégonde, not knowing that she had become ugly, because no one had informed her of it, reminded Candide of his promise in so firm a tone that the good Candide did not dare to refuse her. He then told the Baron that he was going to marry his sister. "I will never put up with," said the Baron, "such baseness on her part and such insolence on yours; no, I never will be reproached for such infamy: why, my sister's children would not even qualify for the first ecclesiastical dignities in Germany;*

---

*In the eighteenth century, certain ecclesiastical orders in Germany and France were open only to nobles.

nor shall a sister of mine ever be the wife of any person below the rank of a baron of the empire." Cunégonde flung herself at her brother's feet, and bathed them in her tears, but he still was inflexible. "You foolish man," said Candide, "I freed you from the galleys, paid your ransom and your sister's, too, who was washing dishes and is very ugly, and yet I condescend to marry her; and will you presume to oppose the match? If I followed the impulses of my anger I would kill you again." "You mayest kill me again," said the Baron, "but you will not marry my sister while I am living."

XXX
Conclusion

Candide had in truth no real desire to marry Miss Cunégonde; but the Baron's extreme impertinence persuaded him to conclude the match; and Cunégonde pressed him so eagerly that he could not back out. He consulted Pangloss, Martin, and the faithful Cacambo. Pangloss composed a fine treatise, by which he proved that the baron had no right over his sister; and that she might, according to all the laws of the empire, marry Candide with the left hand.* Martin thought they should throw the Baron into the sea; Cacambo decided that he must be delivered to the Turkish captain and sent to the galleys, and then they should send him by the first ship to the Father-General in Rome. This advice seemed to be very good: the old woman approved of it, and nothing was said to his sister. The business was executed at a small price; and they had the pleasure of tricking a Jesuit and punishing the pride of a German baron.

It was altogether natural to suppose that after undergoing so many disasters, Candide, who was married to his mistress, and living with the philosopher Pangloss, the philosopher Martin, the prudent Cacambo, and the old woman, and who had also brought home so many diamonds from the country of the ancient Incas, would lead the most agreeable life in the world. But he had been so cheated by the Jews[32] that he had nothing else left but his little farm; his wife, every day growing more and more ugly, became headstrong and insupportable; the old woman was infirm, and more ill-natured even than Cunégonde. Cacambo, who worked in the garden, and carried the produce of it to sell at Constantinople, was

---

*A morganatic marriage; that is, one that grants no equality of rights or privileges to the spouse of lower social rank or his or her offspring.

worn down by this labour, and cursed his fate. Pangloss was in despair at being unable to make a name for himself in any of the German universities. And as to Martin, he was firmly persuaded that things are equally bad everywhere; he endured with patience. Candide, Martin, and Pangloss disputed sometimes about metaphysics and morality. From the windows of the farm they often saw boats passing by carrying effendis, bashaws, and cadis,* into exile on Lemnos, Mytilene, and Erzeroum; and other cadis, bashaws, and effendis were seen coming back to take the place of the exiles, and were then exiled in turn. They saw several heads very curiously impaled upon poles, which were going to be presented at the Sublime Porte.† Such sights gave rise to more discussions: and when they were not arguing, the boredom was so excessive that the old woman ventured one day to tell them, "I would be glad to know which is worse: to be raped a hundred times by negro pirates, to have one buttock cut off, to run the gauntlet among the Bulgarians, to be whipped and hanged at an *auto-da-fé*, to be dissected, to be chained to an oar in a galley; and, in short, to experience all the miseries through which every one of us has passed, or to remain here doing nothing?" "This," said Candide, "is a grand question."

This discourse gave birth to new reflections, and Martin in particular concluded that man was born to live either in the convulsions of misery, or in the lethargy of boredom. Candide did not agree, but he did not provide any other opinion. Pangloss asserted that he had undergone dreadful sufferings; but having once stated that everything went on as well as possible, he still maintained it, and at the same time didn't believe it all.

One thing more than ever confirmed Martin in his detestable principles, made Candide hesitate, and embarrassed Pangloss. It was the arrival of Pacquette and Brother Giroflée one day at their farm. This couple had been in the utmost distress; they had quickly spent their three thousand piastres; they had split up, been reconciled; quarrelled again, been thrown into prison; had made their escape, and at last Brother Giroflée turned Turk. Pacquette still continued to

---

*Turkish titles: An *effendi* is a priest or a scholar, a *bashaw* a military chief or governor of a province, a *cadi* a minor Muslim magistrate or judge.

†Originally the gate to the Sultan's palace where justice was administered.

follow her trade wherever she went; but she made little or no money at it. "I told you," said Martin to Candide, "that your presents would soon be squandered, and would only make them more miserable. You and Cacambo have spent millions of piastres, and yet you are not any happier than Brother Giroflée and Pacquette." "Ah!" said Pangloss to Pacquette, "It is heaven who has brought you here among us, my poor child! Do you know that you have cost me the tip of my nose, one eye and one ear? And look at you now! Eh! What a world!" This new adventure brought them more deeply than ever into philosophical debates.

In the neighbourhood lived a very famous dervish who was thought to be the best philosopher in Turkey; they went to consult him. Pangloss, who was their spokesman, addressed him: "Master, we've come to beg you to tell us why so strange an animal as man has been created."

"Why do you trouble your head about it?" said the dervish; "is it any business of yours?" "But my reverend father," said Candide, "there is a horrible deal of evil on the earth." "What does it matter," says the dervish "whether there is evil or good? When his highness sends a ship to Egypt, does he worry whether the rats in the vessel are at their ease or not?" "What must be done then?" says Pangloss. "Be quiet," answers the dervish. "I had hoped," replied Pangloss, "to reason a little with you on the causes and effects, on the best of possible worlds, the origin of evil, the nature of the soul, and a pre-established harmony." At these words the dervish shut the door in their faces.

During this conversation news was spreading aboard that two viziers of the bench and the mufti had just been strangled at Constantinople, and several of their friends impaled. The catastrophe caused a great stir for some hours. Pangloss, Candide, and Martin, as they were returning to the little farm, met with a good-looking old man, who was enjoying some fresh air at his doorway under an alcove formed of the boughs of orange trees. Pangloss, who was as inquisitive as he was argumentative, asked him the name of the mufti who had just been strangled. "I don't know anything about it," answered the good old man; "I never knew the name of any mufti or vizier breathing. I am entirely ignorant of the event you speak of; I presume that in general some who meddle in public affairs sometimes meet a miserable end, and they deserve it; but I never inquire about what is happening in Constantinople. I am satisfied with sending the produce of my garden there." After saying these words, he invited the strangers to come into his house. His two daughters and two sons presented them with all sorts of sherbet which they had made; as well as caymac heightened with the peels of candied citrons, oranges, lemons, pine-apples, pistachio-nuts, and Mocha coffee untainted with the bad coffee of Batavia or the American islands. After which the two daughters of this good Muslim perfumed the beards of Candide, Pangloss and Martin.

"You must certainly have a vast estate," said Candide to the Turk, who replied, "I have no more than twenty acres of ground, the whole of which I cultivate myself with the help of my children, and our labour keeps us from three great evils—boredom, vice, and want."

Candide as he was returning home made profound reflections on the Turk's discourse. "This good old man," said Martin, "appears to me to have chosen for himself a fate much more preferable to that of the six kings with whom we had the honour to dine." "Human grandeur," said Pangloss, "is very dangerous, if we believe the testimonies of almost all philosophers; for we find Eglon, king of Moab, was assassinated by Aod; Absalom was hung by the hair of his head, and pierced with three darts; King Nadab, son of Jeroboam, was slain by Baaza; King Ela by Zimri; Ahaziah by Jehu; Athalia by Jehoiada; the kings Jehoiakim, Jeconiah, and Zedekiah were enslaved. You know of the deaths of Crœsus, Astyages, Darius, Dionysius of Syracuse, Pyrrhus, Perseus, Hannibal, Jugurtha, Ariovistus, Cæsar, Pompey, Nero, Otho, Vitellius, Domitian, Richard II of England, Edward II, Henry IV, Richard III, Mary Stuart, Charles I, the three Henrys of France, and the Emperor Henry IV."* "I also know," said Candide, "that we must cultivate our garden." "You are right," said Pangloss; for when man was put into the Garden of Eden, he was put there with the idea that he should work the land; and this proves that man was not born to be idle." "Let's work,

---

*All the rulers mentioned in this long list met a terrible death.

then, without disputing," says Martin. "It is the only way to make life bearable."

The little society, one and all, entered into this laudable scheme, and each began to exercise his talents. The little piece of ground yielded a plentiful crop. Cunégonde indeed was very ugly, but she became excellent at pastry-work. Pacquette embroidered, the old woman took care of the linen. Everyone, down to Brother Giroflée, did some service. He was a very good carpenter, and became an honest man. Pangloss sometimes would say to Candide: "All events are linked together in the best of all possible worlds; for, after all, had you not been kicked out of a fine castle for your love of Miss Cunégonde, had you not been put into the Inquisition, had you not travelled across America on foot, had you not stabbed the Baron with your sword, and had you not lost all your sheep which you brought from the good country of El Dorado, then you wouldn't be here eating preserved citrons and pistachio-nuts." "Excellently observed," answered Candide; "but we must cultivate our garden."

ENDNOTES

1. (p. 12) *"everything is best"*: Throughout *Candide*, Voltaire ridicules Leibniz's philosophy; caricaturing and oversimplifying Leibniz's optimism and terminology and presenting obviously comical, trivial, and grotesque examples. Voltaire scoffs at the doctrine that everything in this world exists for a specific and excellent reason.

2. (p. 14) *the Bulgarians*: The Bulgarians represent the Prussian troops of Frederick the Great in the Seven Years War (1756–1763). Voltaire wishes to insinuate that both the soldiers and their leader are homosexuals; the French word *bougre*, like the English *bugger*, derives from the word *Bulgarian*, because of the association of Bulgaria with the medieval sect the Bogomils, who were accused of sodomy.

3. (p. 16) *the Abares*: The name refers allegorically to the French, who were aligned with the Austrians and Russians against the Prussians and British in the Seven Years War. Actually, "Abares" designates a tribe of Scythians, who lived in the steppes near the Black Sea and who might therefore be at war with the Bulgars.

4. (p. 23) *"the law which seizes on the effects of bankrupts, only to cheat the creditors"*: Voltaire had recently sustained a significant financial loss through the bankruptcy proceedings against one of his brokers.

5. (p. 26) *they felt the earth tremble under their feet, and . . . thirty thousand inhabitants . . . were buried beneath the ruins*: The Lisbon earthquake and fire of November 1, 1755, had an enormous impact on Voltaire and was one of the contemporary tragedies that caused him to question Leibniz's philosophical optimism, as especially evident in his eloquent *Poem on the Lisbon Disaster* (1756) and, of course, in *Candide*.

6. (p. 26) *"I . . . have trampled four times upon the crucifix in as many voyages to Japan"*: It was reported that Europeans were allowed to trade in Japan only if they first demonstrated their repudiation of Christianity by trampling on the crucifix.

7. (p. 27) *familiars of the Inquisition*: "Familiars" were undercover agents of the Inquisition who had the power to arrest suspects. Established

in the Middle Ages to suppress heresy, the Inquisition was still active in the eighteenth century.

8. (p. 27) *"you do not believe in free-will"*: Free will versus determinism is widely debated in philosophical and theological circles. Blindly faithful to Leibniz in this respect, as in so many others, Pangloss feebly tries to explain the philosopher's attempt to reconcile metaphysical necessity with his belief in freedom.

9. (p. 28) *an auto-da-fé*: The name—Portuguese for "act of faith"—of a church ceremony consisting of a procession, mass, and burning at the stake of heretics condemned by the Inquisition. An *auto-da-fé* took place in Lisbon on June 20, 1756.

10. (p. 28) *rounded up a Biscayner for marrying his godmother*: Such a marriage was condemned as incest, since the Catholic Church viewed a godmother as a relative.

11. (p. 28) *who while eating a chicken had set aside a piece of bacon used for seasoning*: The two Portuguese men who removed the bacon thereby revealed themselves as converts who still secretly practiced the Jewish religion.

12. (p. 28) *The mitre and san-benito worn by Candide were painted with upside-down flames . . . but Dr. Pangloss's . . . were upright*: The inverted flames on the *san-benito* and mitre worn by Candide signify that he had repented, while the upright flames on Pangloss's outfit indicate an unrepentant heretic. Pangloss, who was the outspoken one in the conversation with the agent of the Inquisition, was probably considered guiltier than Candide, who, as was his habit, merely listened with apparent approval.

13. (p. 32) *seemed to devour her with his eyes all the time she was speaking*: This whole chapter is a parody of a popular novelistic formula of the period for depicting the happiness of lovers reunited after being separated by tragic circumstances.

14. (p. 40) *accused of having excited one of the Indian tribes . . . to revolt against the kings of Spain and Portugal*: An uprising by the natives against their European masters took place in 1755 and 1756, and Jesuit missionaries were accused of inciting it. Spain sent troops to put down the rebellion, and Candide is recruited for this mission.

15. (p. 41) *"I am the daughter of Pope Urban X and of the Princess of Palestrina"*: Among Voltaire's manuscripts found after his death is the following ironical comment on this passage: "Observe the author's extreme discretion. There has never been until now a Pope named Urban X. The author avoided attributing a bastard daughter to a known Pope. What circumspection! What delicacy of conscience!"

16. (p. 46) *he had been sent to the court of the King of Morocco by a Christian prince*: Portugal allied itself with Morocco in order to obtain trading privileges, and the eunuch was sent as an emissary to conclude a treaty.

17. (p. 50) *Robeck*: In 1736 Johann Robeck (1672–1739) published a treatise advocating suicide and soon thereafter drowned himself. The controversial topic of suicide was widely discussed in the eighteenth century.

18. (p. 63) *"let's eat this Jesuit"*: The French phrase "Mangeons du jésuite" caught the popular fancy at a time of rising hostility to the Jesuits, culminating in their expulsion from France in 1764.

19. (p. 80) *Socinian*: The Socinians were a heretical sect organized in the sixteenth century by Lelio Sozzini, or Laelius Socinus (1525–1562), and his nephew, Fausto Sozzini, or Faustus Socinus (1539–1604). The latter settled in Poland after leaving the Roman Catholic Church. Socinianism attempts to reconcile Christianity and humanism by stressing the importance of rational conscience and minimizing the doctrines of the Trinity and the divinity of Christ.

20. (p. 81) *a Manichæan*: A believer in two coequal spirits of Good and Evil struggling to gain the upper hand in the Universe. Mani, or Manicheus, was a Persian philosopher of the third century B.C. who posited a primal struggle between these two opposing and equal forces or principles, one of light and the other of darkness. Manichaeism, which is fundamentally pessimistic, was frequently confused with Socinianism in the eighteenth century, probably because both were heretical. Hence Martin's ironical remark.

21. (p. 88) *"when they die we throw their bodies upon a dunghill"*: This is a reference to the automatic excommunication of actors and actresses by the Catholic Church and to the resultant refusal to bury them in consecrated ground. One of Voltaire's causes was to give actors an honorable status in society and the right to be buried in Christian cemeteries.

22. (p. 88) *"Miss Monimia made her exit . . . in the parish"*: Miss Monimia refers to Adrienne Lecouvreur (1692–1730), a great actress of the Comédie Française much admired by Voltaire; she made her debut in the role of Monine in Jean Racine's tragedy *Mithridate* (1673); after her death she was denied ecclesiastic burial.

23. (p. 93) *"Jansenists against Molinists"*: Jansenists were members of a Catholic sect that sought religious reform and followed the doctrines of Cornelis Jansen (1585–1638), a Dutch theologian who limited free will in favor of predestination and divine grace. His best-known follower was French scientist and philosopher Blaise Pascal (1623–1662). They were condemned as heretical and were fiercely opposed by the Jesuits, or Molinists—from the Spanish Jesuit Luis de Molina (1535–1600), who emphasized free will. The quarrel between the two sects continued well into the eighteenth century.

24. (p. 96) *not like the one in the month of May, 1610, but like the one in the month of December in 1594*: François Ravaillac succeeded in killing Henry IV in

1610, whereas Jean Châtel had failed in his attempt to kill Henry IV in 1594.

25. (p. 99) *Canada is worth*: This is a reference to the struggle for Canada during the Seven Years War (1756–1763). The wars of the French and English over Canada persisted throughout the eighteenth century until the Peace of Paris (1763) confirmed England's conquest. Voltaire failed to appreciate the importance of Canada.

26. (p. 99) *In front of this man stood four soldiers . . . perfectly well satisfied*: Candide witnesses here the historical execution of Admiral John Byng (1704–1757), who was executed by a firing squad, by verdict of a court-martial, for allegedly having neglected his duties and thereby having significantly contributed to the humiliating defeat of the English by the French fleet under La Galissonnière in the battle of Minorca (1756) during the Seven Years War. Voltaire had met Byng during his years of exile in England, considered him an innocent victim of national pride, and unsuccessfully intervened in his behalf.

27. (p. 108) *"But your excellency does not hold the same opinion of Virgil?" . . . "I prefer Tasso and even that sleepy tale-teller Ariosto*: The Roman poet Virgil (70–19 B.C.) wrote the epic poem the *Aenied*; until the nineteenth century, many ranked him above Homer; the Italian poet Torquato Tasso (1544–1595) wrote *Jerusalem Delivered*; the Italian poet Ludovico Ariosto (1474–1533) wrote *Orlando Furioso*.

28. (p. 108) *"May I take the liberty to ask if you do not get great pleasure from reading Horace?". . . . "I see nothing extraordinary in his journey to Brundusium . . . language was dipped in vinegar. His indelicate verses . . . great offence*: Quintus Horatius Flaccus (65–8 B.C.), known as Horace, was one of the greatest Latin poets. The ancient city Brundusium, the modern Brindisi, is located on the heel of the boot of Italy. The phrase "dipped in vinegar" is a reference to a phrase in Horace's *Satires* (satire 1, book 7). "His indelicate verses" is a reference to Horace's *Epodes* 5, 8, and 12.

29. (p. 117) *Ragotsky*: Ferenc II Rákóczi (1676–1735) was a Hungarian prince who, with the support of Louis XIV, led a rebellion against the Austrians and became prince of Transylvania (1707–1711); after several defeats, he fled to Poland, then to France, and eventually to Turkey.

30. (p. 123) *"everything in this world happens for the best . . . pre-established harmony is the finest thing in the world, as well as a plenum and the materia subtilis*": These are all terms of Leibnizian philosophy. The *plenum* and the *materia subtilis* were also theories of René Descartes (1596–1650) to explain that there was no vacuum and that light rays could pass through this "subtle matter." Voltaire was intent on ridiculing these outdated theories in favor of the more advanced views of English mathematician and physicist Isaac Newton (1642–1727).

31. (p. 124) *the contingent or non-contingent events of this world*: Yet another example of Voltaire's use of Leibnizian terminology in order to make fun of Leibniz's philosophy.

32. (p. 126) *he had been so cheated by the Jews*: This amounts to a settling of scores, for Voltaire had incurred significant financial losses as a result of disputes with and bankruptcies of Jewish financiers and bankers.

INSPIRED BY *CANDIDE*

George Bernard Shaw's Candida

The name Candide has come to mean a naive person who is optimistic to the point of stupidity. However, the title character of George Bernard Shaw's play *Candida* (1893) is not at all naive. Shaw speaks of Candida in his stage directions: "Her ways are those of a woman who has found that she can always manage people by engaging their affection, and who does so frankly and instinctively without the smallest scruple. So far, she is like any other pretty woman who is just clever enough to make the most of her sexual attractions for trivially selfish ends: but Candida's serene brow, courageous eyes, and well set mouth and chin signify largeness of mind and dignity of character to ennoble her cunning in the affections."

At *Candida*'s center is a love triangle: Candida; her husband, Morell; and Eugene Marchbanks, a poet of eighteen who plays the role of the naïf. Marchbanks's metaphysical poetry echoes the optimistic theories of Leibniz and Pope that Voltaire had lambasted. Shaw, whose best of all possible worlds was no doubt a socialist one, constructed a drama every bit as subversive and critical of human folly as Voltaire's *Candide*. But by giving Candida the twin gifts of reason and power, Shaw located wisdom in the feminine.

Leonard Bernstein's Candide

The evolution of the comic operetta *Candide* is a story of prolonged adaptation and revision. Leonard Bernstein began work on a musical based on Voltaire's *Candide* in 1954, with help from playwright Lillian Hellman and eventual poet laureate Richard Wilbur. Before the work's 1956 premiere, Bernstein said of Hellman's book: "She has taken Voltaire and done much more than adapt him: she has added,

deleted, rewritten, replotted, composed brand new sequences, provided a real ending, and, I feel, made it infinitely more significant
for our country and our time." To Wilbur's verses were added lyrics
by John La Touche, Dorothy Parker, and Bernstein himself. Bernstein
composed the score, arguably one of the most complex in musical
theater, around the same time that he wrote the bold and sumptuous
West Side Story (1957). When it opened in Boston and had a relatively
short run on Broadway (1956–1957), the two-act *Candide* was not
considered a success; rather than comic, the libretto struck audiences
as angry in its targeting of McCarthyism as the modern corollary of
the Inquisition.

In 1959, the bicentennial of the publication of Voltaire's *Candide*,
Bernstein's musical opened in London with some new songs. This
production did not succeed either, nor did those based on subsequent revisions in 1966, 1967, 1968, and 1971. In 1973 Hellman's
book was abandoned completely in favor of a new one by Hugh
Wheeler, and Steven Sondheim contributed new lyrics. Director
Harold Prince took on the task of taming Bernstein's score, squeez-
ing it into one act and paring down the orchestra to thirteen members. This version, executed without significant input from
Bernstein, was the first to have any success. However, though rol-
lickingly funny from curtain to curtain, the 1973 version had lost
much of the philosophy of the original.

The director of the Scottish Opera, John Mauceri, began work on
his version of the musical in 1982. Mauceri expanded the 1973
version back into two acts and restored nearly all of Bernstein's
music. Five years later, he brought Bernstein back into the process,
and the two collaborated on a 1988 production in Glasgow. After
the death of Hugh Wheeler, the job of expanding the book fell to
John Wells. His revisions reinserted several incidents from Voltaire's
original. In 1989 Mauceri and Bernstein mounted a production in
London that, for the first time, Bernstein conducted himself; it in-
cluded all the favorites from the original 1956 production as well
as songs added later, including "Best of All Possible Worlds," with
the combined lyrics of Richard Wilbur and Steven Sondheim, and
"Glitter and Be Gay."*Candide: Final Revised Version, 1989* is now considered definitive. Harold Prince revived *Candide* for the New York City
Opera in 1994 and 1997.

COMMENTS & QUESTIONS

In this section, we aim to provide the reader with an array of perspectives on the text, as well as questions that challenge those perspectives. The commentary has been culled from sources as diverse as reviews contemporaneous with the work, letters written by the author, literary criticism of later generations, and appreciations written throughout history. Following the commentary, a series of questions seeks to filter Voltaire's Candide *through a variety of points of view and bring about a richer understanding of this enduring work.*

Commentary

FRANCIS ESPINASSE

The civilized world was horrified by the news of the terrible earthquake of Lisbon (November 1, 1755). Strictly considered, this frightful catastrophe was only, on a large scale, what, on a smaller, was, and is, happening every day. A vessel founders at sea, a house or theatre is on fire: the just and unjust alike, parents and innocent children, perish in the waves or in the flames, and there is weeping and wailing in many a home. But the colossal magnitude of the appalling disaster at Lisbon made transcendently more intense that feeling of the problematic in human destiny, which is aroused more or less, in susceptive minds, by the vicissitudes of daily life. Goethe, then a boy of six, was as much perplexed as the sexagenarian Voltaire how to reconcile the goodness of the Deity with the seemingly aimless cruelty of what he had permitted, or ordained, to happen at Lisbon. The "whatever is is right," the "all partial evil universal good," of Pope's famous essay, so much admired by Voltaire, who translated them into the pithy formula:"All is well" (*tout est bien*), were now pronounced by him unsatisfactory. He had opposed a sort of optimism of his own to Pascal's pessimism, and in "Le Mondain" had sung of the pleasures enjoyed by cultivated and civilized man. But he now struck his lyre to a very different tune in his "Poem on the Disaster at Lisbon; or, an Examination of the Axiom, All is Well"—to which he opposed a gloomy catalogue of all the ills that flesh is heir to. . . . Though not printed until some years later, [Candide] was begun soon after the Lisbon earthquake.

—from Life of Voltaire (1892)

LYTTON STRACHEY

The doctrine which [Voltaire] preached—that life should be ruled, not by the dictates of tyranny and superstition, but by those of reason and humanity—can never be obliterated from the minds of men.

—from The New Republic (August 6, 1919)

HENRY MORLEY

Voltaire in Candide, as Johnson in Rasselas, expressed the despair of the time over the problem of man's life on earth. Voltaire mocked and Johnson mourned over the notion that this is the best possible world. Each taught the vanity of human wishes. . . . All evils of life, wittily heaped together in Candide, when they arise from man's fraud and wrong-doing are conquerable in long course of time; and conquest of them means that advance of civilization towards which we have begun to labour in this century, with more definite aims than heretofore. The struggle of the French Revolution to lift men at once above those grosser ills of life which pressed upon them in the eighteenth century, and wrung from them such books as Candide and Rasselas, failed only in its immediate aim. Its highest hope is with us still, quickened though sobered by the failure of immediate attainment. A State can be no better than the citizens of which it is composed. Our labour now is not to mould States but make citizens.

—from Morley's introduction to Candide (1922)

E. M. FORSTER

[Voltaire] wrote enormously: plays (now forgotten); short stories, and some of them still read—especially that masterpiece, Candide. He was a journalist, and a pamphleteer, he dabbled in science and philosophy, he was a good popular historian, he compiled a dictionary, and he wrote hundreds of letters to people all over

Europe. He had correspondents everywhere, and he was so witty, so up-to-date, so on the spot that kings and emperors were proud to get a letter from Voltaire and hurried to answer it with their own hand. He is not a great creative artist. But he is a great man with a powerful intellect and a warm heart, enlisted in the service of humanity. That is why I rank him with Shakespeare as a spiritual spokesman for Europe. Two hundred years before the Nazis came, he was the complete anti-Nazi.

—from *Two Cheers for Democracy* (1951)

Questions

Because God is all-knowing, all-powerful, and all-benevolent, any world He created would have to be the best possible. It is true that there are murders, rapists, thieves, and bloody-minded dictators, but free will is so important a good that evildoers must be allowed to choose to do evil. Similarly, for there to be the maximum amount of order, beauty, and variety in nature, there also has to be the possibility of droughts, earthquakes, volcanic eruptions, and the like. Such, greatly simplified, are the kinds of ideas against which Voltaire directs his satire.

1. Does *Candide* refute such ideas successfully?

2. Could it be that Voltaire's satire is not so much directed against these ideas as against people who use them as a pretext for a heartless and self-righteous complacency?

3. What do you understand Candide to mean when he says that from now on he will "tend his garden"? Refrain from public life? Accept things as they are? Try to expand this phrase into a program for living.

4. What is your own answer to the violence and misery of human life as Voltaire depicts it?

FOR FURTHER READING

Biographical and General Studies

Ayer, A. J. *Voltaire.* New York: Random House, 1986.

Barber, William H. *Leibniz in France from Arnault to Voltaire.* Oxford: Clarendon Press, 1955. Reprint: New York: Garland, 1985.

———. *Voltaire.* London: Arnold, 1960.

Besterman, Theodore. *Voltaire.* New York: Harcourt, Brace and World, 1969.

Bird, Stephen. *Reinventing Voltaire: The Politics of Commemoration in Nineteenth-century France.* Oxford: Voltaire Foundation, 2000.

Bottiglia, William F., ed. *Voltaire: A Collection of Critical Essays.* Englewood Cliffs, NJ: Prentice-Hall, 1968.

Gay, Peter. *Voltaire's Politics: The Poet as Realist.* Princeton, NJ: Princeton University Press, 1959. Second edition: New Haven, CT: Yale University Press, 1988.

Lanson, Gustave. *Voltaire.* 1906. Translated by Robert A. Wagoner; introduction by Peter Gay. New York: John Wiley and Sons, 1966.

Mitford, Nancy. *Voltaire in Love.* New York: Harper, 1957. Paperback edition: New York: Carroll and Graf, 1999.

Sareil, Jean. "Voltaire." In *European Writers: The Age of Reason and the Enlightenment,* edited by George Stade. New York: Charles Scribner's Sons, 1984, pp. 367–392.

Torrey, Norman. *The Spirit of Voltaire.* New York: Columbia University Press, 1938. Reprint: New York: Russell and Russell, 1968.

Wade, Ira Owen. *The Intellectual Development of Voltaire.* Princeton, NJ: Princeton University Press, 1969.

Critical Studies of Candide

Barber, William H. *Voltaire: "Candide."* London: Arnold, 1960.

Bottiglia, William F., ed. *Voltaire's Candide: Analysis of a Classic.* Geneva: Institut et Musée Voltaire, 1959, 1964.

Havens, George R., ed. *Candide.* New York: Henry Holt, 1934.

Mason, Haydn. *"Candide": Optimism Demolished.* New York: Twayne Publishers, 1992.

Wade, Ira Owen. *Voltaire and "Candide": A Study in the Fusion of History, Art, and Philosophy.* Princeton, NJ: Princeton University Press, 1959. Reprint: Port Washington, NY: Kennikat Press, 1972.

Waldinger, Renée, ed. *Approaches to Teaching Voltaire's Candide.* New York: Modern Language Association of America, 1987.

Williams, David. *Voltaire, Candide.* London: Grant and Cutler, 1997.

Look for the following titles, available now from
BARNES & NOBLE CLASSICS

Visit your local bookstore for these and more fine titles.
Or to order online go to: WWW.BN.COM/CLASSICS

Adventures of Huckleberry Finn	Mark Twain	1-59308-112-X	$5.95
The Adventures of Tom Sawyer	Mark Twain	1-59308-139-1	$5.95
The Aeneid	Vergil	1-59308-237-1	$8.95
Aesop's Fables		1-59308-062-X	$5.95
The Age of Innocence	Edith Wharton	1-59308-143-X	$5.95
Agnes Grey	Anne Brontë	1-59308-323-8	$6.95
Alice's Adventures in Wonderland and Through the Looking-Glass	Lewis Carroll	1-59308-015-8	$5.95
The Ambassadors	Henry James	1-59308-378-5	$8.95
Anna Karenina	Leo Tolstoy	1-59308-027-1	$8.95
The Arabian Nights	Anonymous	1-59308-281-9	$9.95
The Art of War	Sun Tzu	1-59308-017-4	$7.95
The Autobiography of an Ex-Colored Man and Other Writings	James Weldon Johnson	1-59308-289-4	$5.95
The Awakening and Selected Short Fiction	Kate Chopin	1-59308-113-8	$6.95
Babbitt	Sinclair Lewis	1-59308-267-3	$8.95
The Beautiful and Damned	F. Scott Fitzgerald	1-59308-245-2	$7.95
Beowulf	Anonymous	1-59308-266-5	$6.95
Billy Budd and The Piazza Tales	Herman Melville	1-59308-253-3	$6.95
Bleak House	Charles Dickens	1-59308-311-4	$9.95
The Bostonians	Henry James	1-59308-297-5	$8.95
The Brothers Karamazov	Fyodor Dostoevsky	1-59308-045-X	$9.95
Bulfinch's Mythology	Thomas Bulfinch	1-59308-273-8	$12.95
The Call of the Wild and White Fang	Jack London	1-59308-200-2	$5.95
Candide	Voltaire	1-59308-028-X	$4.95
The Canterbury Tales	Geoffrey Chaucer	1-59308-080-8	$9.95
A Christmas Carol, The Chimes and The Cricket on the Hearth	Charles Dickens	1-59308-033-6	$6.95
The Collected Oscar Wilde		1-59308-310-6	$9.95
The Collected Poems of Emily Dickinson		1-59308-050-6	$5.95
Common Sense and Other Writings	Thomas Paine	1-59308-209-6	$6.95
The Communist Manifesto and Other Writings	Karl Marx and Friedrich Engels	1-59308-100-6	$5.95
The Complete Sherlock Holmes, Vol. I	Sir Arthur Conan Doyle	1-59308-034-4	$7.95
The Complete Sherlock Holmes, Vol. II	Sir Arthur Conan Doyle	1-59308-040-9	$7.95
Confessions	Saint Augustine	1-59308-259-2	$6.95
A Connecticut Yankee in King Arthur's Court	Mark Twain	1-59308-210-X	$7.95
The Count of Monte Cristo	Alexandre Dumas	1-59308-151-0	$7.95
The Country of the Pointed Firs and Selected Short Fiction	Sarah Orne Jewett	1-59308-262-2	$7.95
Crime and Punishment	Fyodor Dostoevsky	1-59308-081-6	$8.95
Cyrano de Bergerac	Edmond Rostand	1-59308-387-4	$7.95
Daisy Miller and Washington Square	Henry James	1-59308-105-7	$5.95
Daniel Deronda	George Eliot	1-59308-290-8	$9.95

(continued)

Dead Souls	Nikolai Gogol	1-59308-092-1	$8.95
The Deerslayer	James Fenimore Cooper	1-59308-211-8	$10.95
Don Quixote	Miguel de Cervantes	1-59308-046-8	$9.95
Dracula	Bram Stoker	1-59308-114-6	$6.95
Emma	Jane Austen	1-59308-152-9	$6.95
Essays and Poems by Ralph Waldo Emerson		1-59308-076-X	$6.95
Essential Dialogues of Plato		1-59308-269-X	$10.95
The Essential Tales and Poems of Edgar Allan Poe		1-59308-064-6	$7.95
Ethan Frome and Selected Stories	Edith Wharton	1-59308-090-5	$5.95
Fairy Tales	Hans Christian Andersen	1-59308-260-6	$9.95
Far from the Madding Crowd	Thomas Hardy	1-59308-223-1	$7.95
The Federalist	Hamilton, Madison, Jay	1-59308-282-7	$7.95
Founding America: Documents from the Revolution to the Bill of Rights	Jefferson, et al.	1-59308-230-4	$9.95
Frankenstein	Mary Shelley	1-59308-115-4	$5.95
The Good Soldier	Ford Madox Ford	1-59308-268-1	$7.95
Great American Short Stories: From Hawthorne to Hemingway	Various	1-59308-086-7	$9.95
The Great Escapes: Four Slave Narratives	Various	1-59308-294-0	$6.95
Great Expectations	Charles Dickens	1-59308-116-2	$6.95
Grimm's Fairy Tales	Jacob and Wilhelm Grimm	1-59308-056-5	$9.95
Gulliver's Travels	Jonathan Swift	1-59308-132-4	$5.95
Hard Times	Charles Dickens	1-59308-156-1	$5.95
Heart of Darkness and Selected Short Fiction	Joseph Conrad	1-59308-123-5	$5.95
The History of the Peloponnesian War	Thucydides	1-59308-091-3	$11.95
The House of Mirth	Edith Wharton	1-59308-153-7	$7.95
The House of the Dead and Poor Folk	Fyodor Dostoevsky	1-59308-194-4	$9.95
The House of the Seven Gables	Nathaniel Hawthorne	1-59308-231-2	$7.95
The Hunchback of Notre Dame	Victor Hugo	1-59308-140-5	$7.95
The Idiot	Fyodor Dostoevsky	1-59308-058-1	$7.95
The Iliad	Homer	1-59308-232-0	$7.95
The Importance of Being Earnest and Four Other Plays	Oscar Wilde	1-59308-059-X	$6.95
Incidents in the Life of a Slave Girl	Harriet Jacobs	1-59308-283-5	$5.95
The Inferno	Dante Alighieri	1-59308-051-4	$6.95
The Interpretation of Dreams	Sigmund Freud	1-59308-298-3	$8.95
Ivanhoe	Sir Walter Scott	1-59308-246-0	$9.95
Jane Eyre	Charlotte Brontë	1-59308-117-0	$7.95
Journey to the Center of the Earth	Jules Verne	1-59308-252-5	$4.95
Jude the Obscure	Thomas Hardy	1-59308-035-2	$6.95
The Jungle Books	Rudyard Kipling	1-59308-109-X	$5.95
The Jungle	Upton Sinclair	1-59308-118-9	$6.95
King Solomon's Mines	H. Rider Haggard	1-59308-275-4	$7.95
Lady Chatterley's Lover	D. H. Lawrence	1-59308-239-8	$7.95
The Last of the Mohicans	James Fenimore Cooper	1-59308-137-5	$5.95
Leaves of Grass: First and "Death-bed" Editions	Walt Whitman	1-59308-083-2	$11.95
The Legend of Sleepy Hollow and Other Writings	Washington Irving	1-59308-225-8	$6.95
Les Misérables	Victor Hugo	1-59308-066-2	$9.95
Les Liaisons Dangereuses	Pierre Choderlos de Laclos	1-59308-240-1	$8.95
Little Women	Louisa May Alcott	1-59308-108-1	$6.95

(continued)

Lost Illusions	Honoré de Balzac	1-59308-315-7	$9.95
Madame Bovary	Gustave Flaubert	1-59308-052-2	$6.95
Maggie: A Girl of the Streets and Other Writings about New York	Stephen Crane	1-59308-248-7	$8.95
The Magnificent Ambersons	Booth Tarkington	1-59308-263-0	$8.95
Main Street	Sinclair Lewis	1-59308-386-6	$9.95
Man and Superman and Three Other Plays	George Bernard Shaw	1-59308-067-0	$7.95
The Man in the Iron Mask	Alexandre Dumas	1-59308-233-9	$10.95
Mansfield Park	Jane Austen	1-59308-154-5	$5.95
The Mayor of Casterbridge	Thomas Hardy	1-59308-309-2	$7.95
The Metamorphoses	Ovid	1-59308-276-2	$7.95
The Metamorphosis and Other Stories	Franz Kafka	1-59308-029-8	$6.95
Moby-Dick	Herman Melville	1-59308-018-2	$9.95
Moll Flanders	Daniel Defoe	1-59308-216-9	$8.95
My Ántonia	Willa Cather	1-59308-202-9	$5.95
My Bondage and My Freedom	Frederick Douglass	1-59308-301-7	$8.95
Narrative of Sojourner Truth		1-59308-293-2	$6.95
Narrative of the Life of Frederick Douglass, an American Slave		1-59308-041-7	$4.95
Nicholas Nickleby	Charles Dickens	1-59308-300-9	$8.95
Night and Day	Virginia Woolf	1-59308-212-6	$9.95
Nostromo	Joseph Conrad	1-59308-193-6	$9.95
Notes from Underground, The Double and Other Stories	Fyodor Dostoevsky	1-59308-124-3	$8.95
O Pioneers!	Willa Cather	1-59308-205-3	$5.95
The Odyssey	Homer	1-59308-009-3	$5.95
Of Human Bondage	W. Somerset Maugham	1-59308-238-X	$10.95
Oliver Twist	Charles Dickens	1-59308-206-1	$6.95
The Origin of Species	Charles Darwin	1-59308-077-8	$7.95
Paradise Lost	John Milton	1-59308-095-6	$7.95
The Paradiso	Dante Alighieri	1-59308-317-3	$9.95
Père Goriot	Honoré de Balzac	1-59308-285-1	$8.95
Persuasion	Jane Austen	1-59308-130-8	$5.95
Peter Pan	J. M. Barrie	1-59308-213-4	$4.95
The Phantom of the Opera	Gaston Leroux	1-59308-249-5	$6.95
The Picture of Dorian Gray	Oscar Wilde	1-59308-025-5	$4.95
The Pilgrim's Progress	John Bunyan	1-59308-254-1	$7.95
A Portrait of the Artist as a Young Man and Dubliners	James Joyce	1-59308-031-X	$6.95
The Possessed	Fyodor Dostoevsky	1-59308-250-9	$10.95
Pride and Prejudice	Jane Austen	1-59308-201-0	$6.95
The Prince and Other Writings	Niccolò Machiavelli	1-59308-060-3	$5.95
The Prince and the Pauper	Mark Twain	1-59308-218-5	$4.95
Pudd'nhead Wilson and Those Extraordinary Twins	Mark Twain	1-59308-255-X	$7.95
The Purgatorio	Dante Alighieri	1-59308-219-3	$9.95
Pygmalion and Three Other Plays	George Bernard Shaw	1-59308-078-6	$8.95
The Red Badge of Courage and Selected Short Fiction	Stephen Crane	1-59308-119-7	$4.95
Republic	Plato	1-59308-097-2	$6.95
The Return of the Native	Thomas Hardy	1-59308-220-7	$7.95
Robinson Crusoe	Daniel Defoe	1-59308-360-2	$5.95
A Room with a View	E. M. Forster	1-59308-288-6	$5.95
Scaramouche	Rafael Sabatini	1-59308-242-8	$9.95
The Scarlet Letter	Nathaniel Hawthorne	1-59308-207-X	$5.95

(continued)

The Scarlet Pimpernel	Baroness Orczy	1-59308-234-7	$5.95
The Secret Agent	Joseph Conrad	1-59308-305-X	$8.95
The Secret Garden	Frances Hodgson Burnett	1-59308-277-0	$5.95
Selected Stories of O. Henry		1-59308-042-5	$5.95
Sense and Sensibility	Jane Austen	1-59308-125-1	$5.95
Siddhartha	Hermann Hesse	1-59308-379-3	$5.95
Silas Marner and Two Short Stories	George Eliot	1-59308-251-7	$6.95
Sister Carrie	Theodore Dreiser	1-59308-226-6	$10.95
The Souls of Black Folk	W. E. B. Du Bois	1-59308-014-X	$5.95
The Strange Case of Dr. Jekyll and Mr. Hyde and Other Stories	Robert Louis Stevenson	1-59308-131-6	$4.95
Swann's Way	Marcel Proust	1-59308-295-9	$9.95
A Tale of Two Cities	Charles Dickens	1-59308-138-3	$5.95
Tarzan of the Apes	Edgar Rice Burroughs	1-59308-227-4	$7.95
Tess of d'Urbervilles	Thomas Hardy	1-59308-228-2	$7.95
This Side of Paradise	F. Scott Fitzgerald	1-59308-243-6	$6.95
Three Theban Plays	Sophocles	1-59308-235-5	$7.95
Thus Spoke Zarathustra	Friedrich Nietzsche	1-59308-278-9	$7.95
The Time Machine and The Invisible Man	H. G. Wells	1-59308-388-2	$6.95
Tom Jones	Henry Fielding	1-59308-070-0	$8.95
Treasure Island	Robert Louis Stevenson	1-59308-247-9	$4.95
The Turn of the Screw, The Aspern Papers and Two Stories	Henry James	1-59308-043-3	$5.95
Twenty Thousand Leagues Under the Sea	Jules Verne	1-59308-302-5	$5.95
Uncle Tom's Cabin	Harriet Beecher Stowe	1-59308-121-9	$7.95
Vanity Fair	William Makepeace Thackeray	1-59308-071-9	$7.95
The Varieties of Religious Experience	William James	1-59308-072-7	$7.95
Villette	Charlotte Brontë	1-59308-316-5	$9.95
The Virginian	Owen Wister	1-59308-236-3	$9.95
Walden and Civil Disobedience	Henry David Thoreau	1-59308-208-8	$5.95
War and Peace	Leo Tolstoy	1-59308-073-5	$12.95
The War of the Worlds	H. G. Wells	1-59308-362-9	$5.95
Ward No. 6 and Other Stories	Anton Chekhov	1-59308-003-4	$7.95
The Waste Land and Other Poems	T. S. Eliot	1-59308-279-7	$4.95
The Way We Live Now	Anthony Trollope	1-59308-304-1	$10.95
The Wind in the Willows	Kenneth Grahame	1-59308-265-7	$6.95
The Wings of the Dove	Henry James	1-59308-296-7	$9.95
Wives and Daughters	Elizabeth Gaskell	1-59308-257-6	$7.95
The Woman in White	Wilkie Collins	1-59308-280-0	$7.95
Women in Love	D. H. Lawrence	1-59308-258-4	$9.95
The Wonderful Wizard of Oz	L. Frank Baum	1-59308-221-5	$6.95
Wuthering Heights	Emily Brontë	1-59308-128-6	$5.95

BARNES & NOBLE CLASSICS

If you are an educator and would like to receive an
Examination or Desk Copy of a Barnes & Noble Classics edition,
please refer to Academic Resources on our website at
WWW.BN.COM/CLASSICS
or contact us at
BNCLASSICS@BN.COM

All prices are subject to change.